CALL ME BILLY

PATRICK MANLEY

This book is dedicated to the memory of Kathy McCluskey. Pretty as can be, she was a good-hearted girl who asked very little of others. I will miss her.

1

It was two in the afternoon when I heard a horse approach the front of the post office. I stepped out the door. A young rider on a tall grey mare stopped in front of me. He wore a black sombrero and a weather beaten red serape. He stepped off the horse and dropped the reins. He grinned as he walked toward me and reached out his hand.

"Remember me, Robert?"

I tried to get a closer look at the face under the sombrero. He looked to be about fifteen. He was about my height. Maybe five foot nine. He was all arms and legs. He couldn't have weighed more than a hundred and thirty pounds. He had lively blue eyes and a somewhat narrow face. When he smiled, his two upper teeth were exposed. The right front tooth was at an angle.

"You came through here with Heiskell Jones about a month ago."

"William Bonney," he nodded as we shook hands.

"It's good to see you again, William." I remembered how Susan was taken with the good manners of the boy when he had stopped earlier with Mr. Jones. "What brings you up this way?"

"I rode up the Pecos to see Pete Maxwell about a job. Work's a little scarce in these parts. Maxwell said he has plenty of vaqueros. I figured a man who owns a whole town might have some work for a fella. I stopped to see Old Man Chisum on my way out of Seven Rivers, but he wasn't taking on any help, neither."

"So, now what?"

"Well, I may go down around Lincoln and see what I can scare up."

At this point, Susan stepped out of the front door of our small adobe house across the road.

"Hello, William," she cheerfully greeted him as she walked toward us.

"Hello, Maam," the young man took off his sombrero and held it against his chest. His light brown hair was sticking out every which way. "I was hoping to see you folks again."

Susan smiled at the boy, "I was just making

a pot of tea. Would you care to join us."

"That's the most civilized offer I've heard since I left Seven Rivers."

"Well, come in and sit down. We'll have a nice conversion."

Susan looked very attractive in her blue and white dress and her light reddish hair rolled up in back. She was closing in on thirty, but she was one of the finest looking women in these parts. I admired her determination to look her best, even at this lonely crossroads on the Pecos.

The three of us went inside and sat at the small wooden table next to the kitchen.

"What brings you back this way, William?" Susan started her interview as she poured the tea.

"You folks should call me Billy. I was called Billy all my life until my mother took up with a fella named William Antrim. My brother and I knew him as Uncle Billy. She decided it would be less confusing if I were called Henry, which is my middle name. When Mother died two years ago in Silver City and my stepfather went to Arizona to seek his fortune in the silver mines, I decided to go by Billy again. For some reason, I never much liked being called Henry."

"Henry's a perfectly fine name, but we're happy to call you Billy," Susan assured him.

"Are you just passing through?"

"It's a long story." Billy set his hat on the table. He thought better of it and dropped the black sombrero on the plank floor next to his chair. His demeanor was relaxed and friendly. His happy blue eyes and toothy smile made you want to like the boy.

"When I arrived back in New Mexico after the trouble at Fort Grant, I ended up at Apache Tejo. I had no prospects at the time. I happened onto a gang led by Jesse Evans. When Evans learned I could handle a revolver better than anyone in his bunch, he offered me some decent wages to join them. I was in no position to decline.

"Jesse worked mostly for John Kenney. He has a big spread north of Mesilla that he and some lawyer stole from a handful of Mexican families that had grazed the land for many years. Anyway, Jesse and his boys would steal cattle from small outfits in the area and deliver them up to Kenney. They would make raids on the Mescalero Reservation and bring the horses to Kenny or take them over to Roswell and sell them to John Chisum.

"I had left Fort Grant in the company of two Apache scouts whose acquaintance I'd made when I arrived at that settlement. In the winter of '75. There's another long story. Elan and Nitis would only go so far as Apache Tejo because the miners around Silver City were shooting Apaches on sight.

"I made some raids with Evans. The work was easy enough. It put some change in my pocket. One night in early October, we rode into Tularosa. The boys all got liquored up and shot up the town some. On our way out that night, Jesse decides to stop at the home of a fella named Sylvester who had earlier testified against the gang in a court hearing in Mesilla.

"Evans and the others fired shots into Sylvester's house even though his wife and children were inside. Then, for good measure, Evans shot the man's dog. The anger started to rise up in me. I told Evans that this wasn't my line of work. He turned his mount to face me. I could see he was angry. That I would challenge his authority in front of his boys.

"I was ready to settle him. It was his selection. Finally, he says, 'Go on, then.' I backed my horse away from the bunch so I wouldn't take a bullet in the back. When I was certain I was clear, I rode into the hills.

"Jesse is a hard case of the worst stripe. He's a little short fella who keeps his boys in line with fear. He'll kill a man for no good reason.

He could out shoot the whole lot of them, but he couldn't out pull me. He had seen me work with my pistol when we had a shooting contest one day when we were killing time. I could see doubt in his face. Like any blowhard I've ever come across, when you call their bluff, they always back down.

"So I split off from the gang after knowing them for only a few weeks. I figured I'd find my way to Roswell and hit up John Chisum for work. His South Springs Ranch runs all the way up the east side of the Pecos. Maybe a hundred miles. Imagine one outfit needing that much pasture.

"So, I'm headed east. Instead of staying with the main road on the mail route that travels through Lincoln, I decided to short cut through Mescalero country. That was my mistake. I had heard warnings about it, but like so many warnings, I thought I knew better. As I came down over the Guadalupes, I stopped at a creek to fill my canteen.

"The side of the ravine was too steep for my mount. I figured I'd wait until the country leveled out and then let her drink. As I squatted along the creek, I saw four Indians approaching from the other side of the canyon. I figured they couldn't see my horse that was just beneath the rim on the other side. Their trail to the water on the far side of the canyon was an easy grade for their ponies. I made for the brush and followed the creek down to where I found a stand of willows. The rocks were steep behind me where they couldn't come at me from that direction.

"I waited in the trees as they watered their horses. I saw them looking at my tracks and then look down the creek in the direction I was hiding. I figured if they came up toward me, I had five chances for the four of them. I had learned to keep one chamber empty to avoid a misfire. Anyway, I was satisfied with my chances.

"To my consternation, they split up. Two led their horses up the trail that I had come down and the other two went back the way they had come. When they found my mount, I knew they would all wait on the rim and watch for me below. Gone was my horse and my Winchester, which I should have had sense enough to bring with me.

"I waited for night. There was no other plan. For those Apaches, it means nothing to sit for hours and watch for any movement down below. It finally got dark. There wasn't much more than a sliver of a moon that night, which was my good fortune. As I slowly made my way down

11

along the creek, I just knew I was going to step on a fat ol' rattler.

"I followed that creek down for maybe two miles. The canyon had started to level out. I climbed up to the north side and lay flat so I could look west as the sun came up behind me. An hour after sunup, there was no sign of those Apaches so I headed east until I got into the heat of the day. I found a clump of cottonwoods and hid in there so I could get a few hours sleep. You sleep a little jumpy with those Indians looking for you. Even the sound of a bird will snap you awake.

"This went on for three days. I kept walking east. I was so hungry, my head was all balled up. I would think I saw something and pull my revolver. Then my head would clear for a moment and it would just be the wind blowing a bush. I had traded one of Evans' boys a Barlow knife for a pair of boots that wouldn't fit him. As it turned out, they wouldn't fit me, neither. They were too small. They raised blisters all over my feet," Billy laughed. "At that point, if you had offered me Christmas dinner or a new pair of shoes, I couldn't have made the call.

"On the third day my head was playing tricks with me. I kept seeing things that weren't there. If I layed down to rest, I'd start to go to sleep and I would see this picture. I was laying on my back in the tall grass when this crow lands on my chest. He would turn his head this way and that while he looked at me. Then, he'd say, 'Are you dead?' I had to make myself get up and start walking. If I didn't, I would have to answer, 'Yes'.

"Late that night. I saw the lights of a small settlement. At first, I couldn't be sure if it was more tricks. I walked in quiet. There was a candle in the window of this adobe house so I tapped on the door. A fella with a grey beard, who turned out to be Heiskell Jones, came out with a shotgun leveled at my chest. When Maam Jones came through the door with a candle, they surely realized that I was the most hopeless bandit they had ever laid eyes upon," Billy smiled.

"Where did you learn your grammar, Billy?" After five years of teaching, this was Susan's favorite question.

"Well, I went to four years of school in Indiana and two years in Silver City. The sod roof of the school in Wichita fell in. That was the end of school that year. It was my mother who made sure I always had a book in my hand. I was sick a lot as a kid. Anytime I was laid up, Mother would make me read to her.

Newspapers. Farm catalogs. Irish poets. I didn't always get the meaning in those poems, but I learned to like the sound of the words.

"I preferred the dime novels, but she frowned on such weak material. Mother was the sternest teacher of all. She made me do a lot of reading and I learned to like it. When I worked at the Truesdell's hotel in Silver City, I used to get in trouble for sitting in the corner with a book when I should have been swamping out the place. Those books were always the best way to get your mind off things."

"I take the papers from Santa Fe and Las Vegas," I said. "You're welcome to stop by and catch up on the news any time you like."

"That's very generous of you, Robert," Billy nodded with a serious expression. "I believe I may take you up on that proposition."

As Billy sipped his tea, I noticed that his hands were very small. His fingernails were clean and trimmed. The only other hands I had seen like his were those of a card dealer.

When Billy saw me looking at his hands, he grinned, "If these hands were the size of some of these fellas, imagine the hard work that would be expected of me."

"You don't like hard work, Billy?" Susan challenged him. She had grown up watching her father work as many as eighteen hours a day in his tannery.

"It's not that I mind the hard work," Billy explained, "But I feel like I'd be cheating another man out of that work. I'd hate to suffer with that burden."

I laughed out loud while Susan studied the boy.

Billy leaned back in his chair and thought for a moment as he stared at his hands. "Maybe hands are like horses. You could spend your days in front of a plow or a hay wagon or you could try to race a hole through the wind."

Billy enjoyed that idea for a moment, "I can ride with any of them. My Apache friends taught me how to ride like an Indian. They got a good laugh the first time I tried to mount from the left and got bucked off, not knowing the horse was Indian broke and you had to get up on the right.

"Chisum and Pete Maxwell weren't swayed by that information. When I told them I could handle a gun better than any man in the territory and work with either hand, they seemed to doubt me."

"You sound very certain of yourself," Susan wasn't convinced by Billy's high praise of himself.

"I got pushed around a lot as a kid. Mostly, I could talk my way out of any box, but I got real tired of those hard cases. Wichita. Silver City. Fort Grant. When I got my first Army Colt, I practiced with both hands until I could hit a tin cup at eighty yards. I figured that evened things out. I wouldn't have to put up with any more of that gaff.

"Elan and Nitis showed me how to shoot on horseback at a full gallop. Hiding along side my mount and firing under the neck. When I was sixteen, every piece of change I could scratch up went for cartridges. From then on, I figured I didn't have to take any lip from anybody."

Susan refilled our cups. "I have a cousin who works for the government in Santa Fe. He told us if we wanted to get out of Chicago, this was our chance. There was a new school that was set to be built last spring and he had secured a teaching position for me. When we got there in July, we learned that the funding for the school had not materialized. It was fortunate that Sean was able to use his influence to get this job for Robert at the new post office that was set to open here at Sunnyside."

"You wouldn't like Chicago, Billy," I said. "We Irish are not entirely well thought of in that city. One fellow running for mayor would get all lathered up and shout out in his stump speech, 'Hang every Irishman from a lamp post.' Most of the crowd favored that idea. We were happy to get out of Chicago, school or no school.

"Susan's father owns a tannery about a quarter mile from the Union Stockyards. At any one time, they may have as many as five thousand head of livestock waiting for slaughter. On a hot summer day, I swear to God, the stench would buckle your knees.

"There was a little stream that ran between the stock pens and Joe's tannery. Bubbling Creek, it's called. The only thing bubbling in that creek were dead carcasses. If the water was low, you could walk right across it.

"Joe Finnegan saw a fine future for me in his tannery. When I took a job with the Chicago News and Mail, it wasn't for any love of the written word. I didn't intend to spend the rest of my days scraping hides. On that score, I share your sentiments, Billy. I'll leave that job to another man," I laughed while Susan gave me a stern look.

"What are your roots, Billy," Susan continued the examination of her new pupil.

"My mother's family landed in New York during the famine. She married a man named,

17

William Bonney. William Henry Bonney. He gave me his name. They decided to leave New York and settle in Indiana. They had no sooner got to Indiana when a wall fell over and killed him. My father was a carpenter.

"Mother then met a fella named Michael McCarty and along comes my younger brother, Josie. So McCarty joins an Indiana volunteer brigade for the signup bonus. He never came back. I always heard he was killed in the battle of Chickamauga.

"Mother was in quite a struggle. She took a job in a laundry, which paid for a small room for Josie and me and her to live. It wasn't too long before she took up with a humorless fella named William Antrim. Uncle Billy, we called him. He helped Mother in many ways, so Josie and I learned to ignore his sour disposition.

"They decided there was an opportunity for cheap land in Kansas. We loaded a wagon and off we went. When we got to Wichita, it wasn't much more than a scattering of frame houses along a muddy street. There were no trees to speak of. I suppose they'd all been cut down to build the town.

"Mother started her own laundry business and Uncle Billy built a cabin a ways out of town. It was a nice tract of land with enough

18

timber to build the cabin and put up some rail fence. It was a fine place for Josie and me to run loose. In the summer, we would walk out to the Arkansas River and swim to an island that was close off the bank. We built a shelter and became pirates for most of the summer. Nothing to do but swim and lay in the shade.

"Everything was going fine in Wichita. Mother bought a number of lots in town. Uncle Billy built mother cabin near his. We moved from above the laundry out to the new cabin. After about a year, Mother started to cough and it only got worse. She still would sing and tell her jokes, but she would get tired and have to lay down.

"They decided Denver would be a better place for her to nurse her cough. They sold off all their property and loaded up a wagon for Denver. We were there only for the winter. We learned that Denver was every bit as cold as Indiana or Kansas. That's when they decided that Santa Fe might be the ticket."

"It couldn't have been any worse that Chicago," I said. "That wind in January comes in off the lake and cuts you to the bone. In the summer, if you're downwind of the stockyards, the smell will make a strong man falter."

"If you're talking stink," Billy grinned, "I'll

19

see your Chicago and raise you Wichita. They would stack those buffalo hides at the west end of town. You could barely see the hides for a cloud of bluebottle flies. Also, the folks there would throw their garbage into the street for the hogs. On a hot day, if the wind was down, you could lose your breakfast."

"When Sean wrote us about the teaching position," I explained, "we didn't deliberate for long before we loaded our wagon for Santa Fe."

"Well," Billy continued, "We headed south for Santa Fe where Uncle Billy had a sister. I swear, from the time I set foot in that pretty little town, I knew I was going to like New Mexico. There was music in the plaza in the evening with the Mexican guitar players singing their serenades in Spanish. The food was like nothing I ever tasted. From then on, it was nothing but chili and frijoles for me."

"You must miss your mother," Susan suggested.

I gave Susan a frown across the table, but she was focused on Billy.

"She was a fine woman. Everyone would tell you so. She always had a joke or a funny tale to tell. She'd make friends quicker that anyone you ever saw. She'd feed strangers who were down on their luck. All my friends in Silver City would run straight to our cabin after school for cookies. Everything was just a laugh and a joke with my mother.

"She was still funny, even after she got real sick. Antrim was away, but she would cook and keep house for me and Josie. I'd hold her hand when she went into those long coughing spells. Near the end, she was spitting out blood. I could see she wasn't going to make it. I figured it might come as a relief for her to get out of all that suffering. The day we buried her, Josie and I went our opposite ways.

"I like to think of her at the dances. She never missed a dance until she got too sick. She'd spin me around the floor. She always had the best steps. I learned them all. Folks would stand to the side and watch her and me go. When she couldn't get to the dances anymore, it seemed to mark the end of any cheer in the family. You might say, it was down hill from there.

"Antrim was away most of the time. Off prospecting. He farmed me and Josie out to work in Silver City. With one family and then anther. He didn't show up for Mother's burial. Most of the rest of the town did. Everyone who knew her would tell you she was a real fine lady. And the best teller of stories."

21

I figured that Susan had put Billy through enough questioning for one afternoon. "My mother and younger sister died of the typhoid in Chicago. It's not easy to sit by someone in the family and know they might not pull through."

"Anyway, you have to get on with it," Billy concluded. "Like they say, it's a long road with no turning back. Mother used to say, 'If you are well spoken and well mannered, you can go a long way in this world.' I doubt she had Fort Sumner in mind."

"Why don't you stay for supper," Susan didn't seem to be finished with our new friend.

"No, I couldn't impose," Billy reached down to pick up his hat. "I have to get back to Fort Sumner."

"It's no imposition."

"Thanks for the tea," Billy gave Susan his best smile. "It brought back some fine memories. It was real nice to talk with you folks. I suppose you not getting that teaching job in Santa Fe was my good fortune. I haven't met anyone as educated as yourselves since I left Silver City. I thank you again."

Billy stood up and I followed him out the door. When we got outside, I realized that he hadn't tied his horse.

"Aren't you worried she'll run off?"

"Gracie's a very intelligent filly," Billy said as he looked into the horse's eyes and stroked her neck. "More intelligent that some people I could name. We keep an eye out for one another."

"Thanks for stopping by, Billy. You're welcome here any time. You can catch up on the newspapers."

"That's kind of you, Robert. I didn't want to say so inside, but there's a card game waiting at Beaver Smith's saloon."

"Good luck, then."

Billy smooched to his filly. She turned her left side toward him. He quickly mounted and turned south. With a wave of his sombrero, he was off at a gallop.

2

The day after Billy sipped tea with us, I received word that there was postal equipment waiting to be picked up at Puerto de Luna. I decided to see if Billy would be willing to go back into the freight business for a couple of days. I figured he could use a piece of change.

When I arrived at Fort Sumner, I went to the parade grounds. It was a clear afternoon in late October. I spotted Billy at the far end of the plaza in front of Beaver Smith's saloon. He was in the company of two Hispano sheepherders.

As I approached, I could see that Billy was doing most of the talking. He was stretched out on his side, lolling in the sun. The two Mexican men sat facing him. The three would laugh and Billy would go on with his story. As I got closer, I could hear that Billy was speaking

Spanish. When I reached them, all three stood up. Billy reached out his right hand.

"Good to see you, Robert," he smiled. "I'd like you to meet my good friends. This is Oscar Gallegos and this is Hector Montoya. El es Roberto O'Dell."

I shook hands with the two leather-faced men. Their hands were hard and calloused from a life of work outdoors. They looked at me carefully for any hint of disrespect. I had learned that if you were honest with the Hispano people and showed them respect, they would support you in any way they could.

"Billy, I could use your help for a couple of days. I need to pick up a wagon and some equipment at Puerto de Luna and bring it back to Sunnyside."

"You know that's my stock and trade," Billy grinned. "When do we leave?"

"If we leave at first light tomorrow, we should make it to Padre Polaco's store by nightfall. With luck, we could be back here the following night."

"As you can see," Billy put his arms out with his palms upward, "I have a lot of responsibilities here at the fort. I s'pose they could get by without me for a few days."

"Alright," I laughed. "I'll see you at

25

daybreak."

"I'll be there," Billy said.

"Nice to meet you," I tipped my hat to Billy's friends.

The next morning, I stepped out the front door of our little adobe as the rooster across the road began to crow. Jesus Velasquez had helped me build a tall coyote fence so our chickens wouldn't disappear each night. Fresh eggs were a luxury out here at the crossroads.

I turned and there was Billy sitting on the bench in front of the post office. Gracie stood next to him with the reins dangling.

"Get any sleep?" I wondered if he had been up gambling all night.

"Barney Mason separated me from my last two dollars, so I turned in early."

"That's a tough way to make a living," I suggested as I walked toward the stable behind the post office to saddle my horse. This had once been a Butterfield stage station. The government had purchased the buildings and the stable to serve as a post office.

"You know, I went up to South Springs to try to get work with Old Man Chisum. Then I rode half way up the Pecos to find work with Pete Maxwell. When it comes to earning a dollar, the pickings are slim around here."

I cinched my saddle and mounted up. Billy's grey mare had followed him to the stable. With a quick leap, he was in the saddle. We headed north up the river road.

"There were things I couldn't say in front of Susan that you ought to know. If we're going to partner up," Billy sounded reluctant. "About that trouble at Fort Grant.

"When mother was laid to rest in Silver City, I moved into the Exchange Hotel on Hudson Street. The Truesdells had bought the old Star Hotel and cleaned it up. I waited tables and washed dishes to pay for my keep. Josie had been farmed out to Joe Dyer at the Orleans Club where he mostly ran errands.

"After the restaurant closed each night, I cleaned up the dining room and swamped out the place. I quit going to school because of the late hours. After my chores were finished, I'd go over to the Orleans and watch the gamblers. I picked up the card games pretty quick. A fella named Sombrero Jack staked me one night and I got to where I was mostly winning.

"Jack took me under his wing and showed me all the tricks and how to know the odds. I had one considerable edge. Those men across the table were generally cross-eyed on whiskey. I would never take a drink. I still won't touch

27

the rotgut. I figure that's a sizable edge. I watched too many miners lose their wages at the tables when they were too drunk to stand up straight.

"So one night, Jack says he has a favor he would ask of me. He's the best friend I had at the Orleans so I figure I couldn't say no. The scheme was that I would stand watch across the street one night while he robbed the Chinese laundry. I knew I wasn't going to prosper much from the affair, but it was something you would do for a friend.

"Charley Sun was the owner of the business and he was pretty well hated around Silver City. He had married a miner's widow who was in a desperate way and a year later, Sun is going around town bragging about how he was going to have a child with this woman. He was buying drinks all over town.

"On his way to Silver City, Sun was almost killed by Apaches. He said was wounded fourteen times. 'Fowteen time', he would say. He would point out his scars and say, 'They killa me here. They killa me here. They killa me here. Sun wasn't a bad Chinaman until he crossed the line one night.

"When the baby was born, it turned out to be a nigger baby. Nobody knows how it happened, but Sun was mad as a hornet. He waits until dark and goes down and feeds the baby to the hogs. There was talk all over town whether a Chinaman could be charged with killing his wife's nigger baby.

"Charley Sun never went to jail, but from then on, all the kids in town were allowed to throw rocks at him. They told us to rock him and run him out of town. Of course, along with the rocks, he got all the clever remarks like, 'You betta like duck!' If he had to leave his laundry, he'd carry a fry pan, which he would hold along side his head. All up the street, you could hear ping, ping, ping, as the rocks hit the fry pan.

"One afternoon, somebody caught Sun in the head with a good size rock. We knew who heaved the rock, but none of us would say. Sun fell to the ground and started to shake all over. He died right in front of his laundry. The folks in Silver City were happy to see him gone after what had happened to that baby.

"Anyway, my end of the robbery was a revolver and gun belt. I had intended to use my winnings at the Orleans to purchase a similar outfit. I was then living at a boarding house run by Mrs. Brown. She found the gun under my bed and reported her findings to Sheriff

Whitehill. Sombrero Jack had skinned out, so I was left to face the charges.

"They put me in a cell that was so dang small, you had to stretch out corner ways to get some sleep. Just a blanket and a dirt floor. I was told the circuit judge wouldn't be in town until December, which was three months down the road. I figured I couldn't last all those days in that iron box. I was no more than a monkey in a cage.

"The sheriff was the father of two of my best friends, Harry and Wayne Whitehill. He had taken over the post when Sheriff McIntosh burned the breeze with three thousand dollars of county tax money. I finally talked Mr. Whitehill into letting me stretch out my legs in the hallway each morning.

"They would lock me in the hallway and I would pace back and forth and try to figure a way out of that lock up. There was a fireplace at the far end of the room. One morning, I got to looking up that shaft and figured I might be able to claw my way out of there. I dug out some handholds and squeezed my way up the chimney.

"I had gained my freedom, but I was covered in soot. I looked like one of those black-faced fellas in the minstrel show. Anyway, I made my way to the river and cleaned up as best I could. I headed for the Truesdells' house where I figured I could get some clean clothes and make my way out of town that night. I had no prospect other than that.

"Mrs. Truesdell did me one better than I could have expected. She was a kind woman and a good friend of my mother's. I had worked under her at the Exchange Hotel before she began to have difficulties with her husband. That's when I moved into Mrs. Brown's boarding house.

"Mrs. Truesdell made me a bath and fixed me up with a set of Chauncey's clean clothes. She had me stay the night in Chauncey's bed and made him sleep on the floor. He groused about that all night. The next morning, she put me on the stage to Clifton with six dollars and a lunch to eat on the way. How's that for a friend?

"When I got to Clifton that evening, I asked around the camp and found my stepfather. Antrim. I was hoping he could point me to some kind of work. He bought me dinner and everything seemed to be going fine. When he heard the story of my trouble with the law and my escape up the chimney, he told me I'd have to get out in the morning. Well, that was that, you might say.

"I stayed in his tent that night, but I didn't get a minute of sleep. I tossed around and considered my prospects. I couldn't return to Silver City and I didn't know anyone in Arizona. I still had the six dollars so I knew I could eat for a few days. I got up before daylight and stole his Army Colt and gun belt and headed south. If he wouldn't help me, I figured I'd help myself.

"Antrim and my situation had gone sour when I came home one afternoon and found him beating my mother. She was on the floor and hollered for me to get out. I couldn't turn my back on her while she was getting beat that way. I raised a chair over my head and whacked Antrim over the back. He let out a yell and collapsed.

"I thought maybe I had killed him. I cleared out of the house after that. I was on the dodge around town for three days until he went out prospecting. I tell you, Robert, to this day if I see a woman or kid being beat, I just see black. My anger comes up and I can't get ahold of it. I've watched folks suffer these mean bastards all my life. I won't stand aside anymore.

"For two years after I got run off from Clifton, I worked with that revolver until no one could out pull me or out shoot me. I'm talking

32

either hand. I decided from then on that anyone who beats a woman or a child is going to get what's coming to him. You agree? Or a horse, for that matter."

We rode along in silence for a few minutes. The sun had just come up in the east. A red-tailed hawk was at work, high over the grassy plain. It glided effortlessly on the breeze with its wings tilting this way and that. The air was so sweet and clean that you couldn't breathe enough of it. It seemed that New Mexico was always blue sky.

The young fella riding along side me was unlike any seventeen year old I had ever known. It was clear that he had gotten his humor and friendly nature from his mother. I would liked to have known her. Another thing was clear. Her passing had sent this boy on a dangerous journey.

"Darling, I am growing old," Billy broke into song.

> *Silver threads among the gold,*
> *Shine upon my brow today,*
> *Life is fading fast away."*

Billy stared ahead as he continued his song. He looked as if he were lost in thought and all alone. He had a fine tenor voice and hit all the proper notes.

But, my darling you will be,
Always young and fair to me,
Yes, my darling, you will be,
Always young and fair to me.

Billy continued through the song with all the choruses. It seemed odd that he would be so sentimental about two people growing old. Maybe, he regretted that his mother had not had the chance to live out her life. Anyway, Billy felt tender about the song and he sang it well.

We rode along for a while without talking. Billy looked even younger than his years atop his tall grey mare. His expression was more serious than before.

"I went up to the Sierra Bonita after I left Clifton. I got on with John Hookers' outfit. I worked on the chuck wagon through the winter. It was a fine time joking with the boys and the food was good. For some reason, Bill Whelan, that was Hooker's foreman, had it in for me. I never saw that big Irishman smile. I figured he had left his humor behind in Tipparrary, which is where he haled from. He couldn't reconcile the notion that you could work and laugh at the same time.

"From there, it was down the mountain to Fort Grant. There was a little settlement a few miles from the army outpost. Robert, that was the most miserable place I ever struck. The soldiers from the fort would come into town to gamble and spend their pay on the whores at the Hog Ranch. There were fights nearly every night and a fair number of killings.

"It was at Fort Grant that I met a little Scotsman named John Mackie. He was retired cavalry. In a shorter time than it takes me to tell it, Mackie and me were separating those drunken soldiers from their saddles and bridles and selling them to a cholo named Benavidez who delivered them into Mexico. It was nothing more than pocket change, but there was no other prospect for wages in that little village.

"While I was in the army transport business, you might call it, I would lay up with my two Apache friends who made camp along the river below town. They weren't allowed in the saloons so I'd bring them the worst kind of red eye you could ever imagine. We had nothing but time to kill while we spent our days in the shade along the river.

"Elan and Nitis showed me how to fight Indian fashion, along side my mount. They showed me how to pick up a handkerchief off

35

the ground, riding at a full gallop. The laugh was on me the first time I tried to mount one of their ponies and got throwed off. Of course, the mare was Indian broke. I learned to speak fairly good Apache while I spent my days in camp with Elan and Nitis.

"Mackie and me had a pretty good run moving that army issue, but the soldiers were onto us. I decided to skin out for Globe City. I figured I was out of harm there, but I was wrong. I was eating a plate of frijoles at a small cantina when up walks a constable, named Duffy. He shows me some papers from Fort Grant and takes me off to jail.

"Beings we were both Irish, Duffy treated me real fair. The lock up in Globe City was nothing but one large holding cell. One night, while the deputy was trying to separate two drunken miners who were clawing and gouging each other on the floor, I just walked out of that jail, easy as pie.

"I walked to the edge of town and found a place to curl up in an alley until morning. I planned on finding a horse and then heading back east. Right around daylight, I wake up to somebody kicking me in the boot. I'll be damned if it wasn't Duffy.

"You get lost?" he says.

"It looks like I've been found," I say as I try to clear my head.

"Duffy laughs and says, 'C'mon, kid.' "

"He marches me back to jail, but all the way there, we're talking about this and that like two old friends. Duffy was a fine humored Irishman. He laughed at all my conversation. He then informs me that he will have to transport me back to Fort Grant the next day.

"He gets me up early the next morning and buys me breakfast at the cafe. He's interested in hearing about Silver City and my mother and Charley Sun. He laughs at my tales all through the meal. Here I was his prisoner, but he's treating me more like we were kin.

"So, we get over to the livery and he shows me my mount for the trip to Fort Grant. If this swayback gelding wasn't twenty, he wasn't a day. Duffy notices the look on my face and laughs real loud."

"Beats walking," he says.

"Walking might get me there quicker," I say.

"C'mon, kid," he laughs "Cinch up."

"We head east up the road and I'm pondering if my mount is likely to make the trip. I'm certain he can't run and I doubt that he can so much as trot. When we reach a place called Cedar Springs, Duffy says he has some business to tend to and walks down to the creek. He leaves me up on the road on my swayback.

"Don't you run off," he laughs as he walks down to a clump of willows.

"As he's standing maybe fifty feet away, he waves me goodbye. So I shake the reins on my bag of bones and start up the road. I can hear Duffy laughing as I get out of sight. I keep looking back, but he never comes after me. I'll never know if he didn't want to make the long ride to Fort Grant or he just wanted to do me a good turn. I'd like to thank him properly and buy him a beer one day.

"When I got to Nitis and Elan's camp, they had a good laugh at what I rode in on. Truth is, I'll always be grateful to that old gelding. He was calm and willing. He delivered me where I needed to get.

"I asked Elan to go find Mackie. I told that cocky little Scotsman that the jig was up. We had to make amends for our trouble with the army. He agreed to return five horses to Fort Thomas to the north. We thought that would square things with the government and we could get on with it.

"After we delivered the horses, we figured we were in the clear at Fort Grant. Me and Mackie wanted to celebrate over a good breakfast at the Hotel de Luna, which was owned by Miles Wood, who was also the constable. I had worked as a cook and dishwasher at the hotel in my early days at Fort Grant so I figured me and Wood were on good terms.

"To our surprise, Wood serves us our breakfast with a pistol under the tray and tells us we're under arrest. We tried to explain that we had returned the horses to Fort Thomas, but he said he had no information of that and he was under orders to arrest us. There went breakfast.

"He takes us out and marches us on foot the three miles to the fort where we're thrown in the stockade. While I waited to learn my fate, they brought in a blacksmith to fit me with bracelets and leg irons. This blacksmith, Frank Cahill, who was working over us, was a blowhard of the worst order. 'Windy,' they called him because he couldn't shut his big mouth for as much as a minute.

"While he fit me with my chains, Cahill poked and prodded me and called me every black name a man could call another man. When I told him he was a lousy son-of-a-bitch, he spat in my face. I told him he would one day regret that. He then yanked on my leg irons and went to kicking me in the back until the guard

39

pulled him off. I'm not inclined to excuse a thing like that.

"That night, a private, named O'Leary, dropped a cold chisel and a hammer on the ground next to me. I had lent three dollars to him a few months earlier to get him out of a jam. I waited until the guard checked on me before I went to work on the leg irons. I could always get out of the bracelets as they were made for fellas with bigger hands."

At this point, we came upon a herd of antelope on the east side of the road. Billy smooched his mare and off they went after those antelope. Billy was down on the neck of the horse with his hands up at the bridle. That tall grey mare was narrowing the distance as she flew over the shin high grass. As she leveled off at a full gallop, her feet seemed to barely touch the ground. She covered the distance effortlessly with Billy's head right on her neck. After about a quarter of a mile, Billy let her ease to a trot.

When Billy got back to the road, he broke into a big smile, " Ain't she something, Robert?"

"She's a beauty to watch," I had to agree. "She makes it look easy."

"Gracie's an actual race mare," Billy explained. "I've already picked up a fair piece of change with her. Nothing in these parts can beat her going longer than a quarter mile. If she doesn't blow out every few days, she starts to get a little sour."

3

The sun was straight up noon. We decided to rest the horses and eat the lunch that Susan had made for us. We sat in the shade of a huge cottonwood tree along the river. Billy attacked the biscuits and ham and hard-boiled eggs as if someone might take the food away from him. It was worth the price of admission to watch him stuff an entire hard-boiled egg in his mouth and swallow it a few seconds later. It occurred to me that the reason he was so thin was that he had missed a lot of meals since he left Silver City.

Two magpies landed on the ground in front of us. They hopped about and hoped for a little something. 'Cheet. Cheet.' I tossed a few scraps of food their way. When Billy had cleaned up his meal, he stretched out his legs with his head against the base of the tree. He looked content as he continued his unlikely tale.

"After O'Leary helped me get free of the stockade, I was fortunate enough to get work with a forage contractor named Sorghum Smith. He ran a hay operation for the army near Fort Thomas. I worked odd jobs for six weeks and got an advance on the next week's pay. I bought a clean set of clothes and an Army Colt at the post trader's.

"You may recall, I had some unfinished business at Fort Grant with that loudmouthed blacksmith. When someone spits in your face, you are not inclined to forget. I went into McDowell's store and had a beer. Then I went across to George Atkin's saloon. Sure enough, there was Cahill. Liquored up and talking over the whole crowd. I walked up to the bar and ordered a beer.

"As soon as Cahill spots me, he marches up and says, 'Now look at the little pimp, will ya'

"I turn to face him and say, 'You lousy old son-of-a-bitch.' He doesn't know I have the .45 tucked under my shirt.

"He says, 'It's the same little pisspot who broke out of the stockade,' and with that, he smacks me up side my head. I take a few steps back and tell him, 'I'm tired of that big mouth of yours.'

"With this, he rushes me and grabs me in a

bear hug and knocks me to the ground. He sits on top of me and commences to smack me in the head. The whole time he's on top of me, he's drooling onto my face. I reach under my shirt and work the pistol free and shoot him in the gut. When I roll out from under him, I see he's shot bad.

"I wasn't about to wait for the law to arrive, so I made for the front door and jumped on a horse owned by a gambler I know. Nobody is going to catch me on that race pony as I ride across the river and into the hills. I laid low for two days until I was sure things had died down. I asked Nitis to deliver the horse back to John Murphy. He was the owner of the horse. When Nitis gets back, he tells me that Cahill is dead and they're after me for murder.

"My two Indian friends got me a horse and agreed to ride with me through Indian country as far as Apache Tejo. Geronimo was causing considerable trouble in the settlements at the time. That's the last I ever saw of Arizona Territory and I can't say I miss it any. It had been touch and go for two years around Fort Grant. I never did gain any level of comfort during my stay down there.

"Some weeks later, I ran into a fella, named Gus Gildea, in Mesilla. He had been at George

Atkin's place that night when I sent Cahill on his trip to hell. Gildea told me I could have made a good case for self-defense. I told him I wasn't about to wait around and see how that hand would play out.

"My mother once told me that if I ever broke the law, I might hang before I turned twenty one. I wasn't in a hurry to give her warning any chance to prevail. Anyway, that's what all this is leading up to. You're riding with a fella who's wanted for murder in Arizona."

I studied Billy as I finished my lunch. Here was a kid of seventeen who was already on the run for a hanging offense. I couldn't say that Cahill did not get what was coming to him, but Billy did not seem overly troubled by the event. He reported the death of the blacksmith as he had told the story of the Chinaman. He seemed to have little sentiment for death in either case.

We mounted up and set off up the sandy road with blue sky in all directions. I thought about how quickly the cold could come to Chicago in the fall. The wind would come in off the lake and the weather would be nasty until April. In New Mexico, fall was a time when you often didn't need to wear a coat.

Billy seemed content with his full belly. As we rode north up the road, he again broke into song. This time, he entertained the prairie with an Irish ballad.

Oh, it's of a brave young
highwayman, this story I will tell.
His name was Willie Brennan and in
Ireland he did dwell.
Twas on the Kilworth Mountains he
commenced his wild career,
And many a wealthy noble before him
shook with fear.

And it's Brennan on the Moor,
Brennan on the Moor,
Bold, brave and undaunted was
young Brennan on the Moor.

One day upon the highway as young
Brennan he went down,
He met the Mayor of Cashel a mile
outside of town,
The Mayor he knew his features and
he said, young man, said he,
Your name is Willie Brennan, you
must come along with me.

And it's Brennan on the Moor,
Brennan on the Moor,
Bold, brave and undaunted was
young Brennan on the Moor.

Now Brennan's wife had gone to

town, provisions for to buy,
And when she saw her Willie, she
commenced to weep and cry.
She said, hand me that tenpenny, as
soon as Willie spoke,
She handed him a blunderbuss from
underneath her cloak.

And it's Brennan on the Moor,
Brennan on the Moor,
Bold, brave and undaunted was
young Brennan on the Moor.

Then with this loaded blunderbuss,
the truth I will unfold,
He made the Mayor to tremble and
robbed him of his gold.
One hundred pounds was offered for
his apprehension there,
So with his horse and saddle for the
mountains he did repair.

And it's Brennan on the Moor,
Brennan on the Moor,
Bold, brave and undaunted was
young Brennan on the Moor.

Now Brennan being an outlaw, upon
the mountains high,
With cavalry and infantry to take him
they did try.
He laughed at them with scorn, until
at last twas said,

By a false-hearted woman, he was
cruelly betrayed.

And it's Brennan on the Moor,
Brennan on the Moor,
Bold, brave and undaunted was
young Brennan on the Moor.

Billy appeared to be satisfied with his latest command performance. I imagined that every antelope within a mile of us had quit grazing and every prairie dog had quit digging as they raised their heads to learn the source of these mellow tones.

"So," I said, "Willie Brennan, tis it?"

"Pray tisn't," Billy smiled. "Young Brennan, he was hanged."

"Betrayed by a woman."

Billy shook his head slowly, "I never intend to meet with that end."

"You'd better be careful," I needled my young friend. "You don't want another visit from that crow."

"I never want to see that damn bird again," Billy looked upset. "He was there to peck out my eyes. Before the others flew in to pick the carcass clean."

It was clear that the image to the crow still troubled Billy. I should not have brought it up.

"No woman would ever betray a fella with such a fine tenor voice."

Billy thought for a moment, "Voice or no, if that crow pays me another visit, I fear it will mean the end." He looked over the prairie as he rode for a while. "You know, Robert, I do hope to see her again one day. That's if I can do enough good deeds to get there."

It seemed that Billy might never get over the passing of his mother. She was the best part of who he was. Now, if he could figure out how to stay alive in this dangerous territory, this likeable kid might go on to enjoy a good life.

As we came through a draw in the mesa, we were finally in sight of Puerto de Luna. The little valley was a circle of green pasture surrounded by red rock mesas. The forty-mile trip from Sunnyside had passed quickly with Billy telling his stories and chasing the occasional herd of antelope.

We decided to water the horses before we reached the small settlement. While they drank from the river, Billy got some things out of his bedroll and went a ways down stream from the horses. He used a bar of soap to wash his face and teeth. He used his wet hands to clean back his sandy hair before he carefully put on the black sombrero.

"There are some pretty girls in Puerto de Luna. I noticed when Heiskell Jones and I passed through here a few weeks ago," Billy explained as he mounted up.

"You noticed, huh?" I was amused by how serious the kid was about making a good impression, "There are some things you'll leave to chance, but looking your best for the ladies isn't one of them."

"You always want to place the odds in your favor," Billy agreed. "That's what I learned from Sombrero Jack before he landed me in jail," Billy laughed. Apparently, there were no hard feelings over the failed burglary at the Chinese laundry.

It was dusk as we trotted into the scattered village of Puerto de Luna. There were about twelve small adobe buildings clustered around a dirt plaza. A large adobe church with a freshly painted white cross was at one end of the square. A long mercantile was at the other end. This was Alexander Grzelachowski's place. He was known in these parts as Padre Polaco.

I dismounted and tied my horse to the rail in front of the store. Billy draped his reins over the rail, but did not tie Gracie. The whitewashed storefront was about eighty feet long with a wooden porch. There was a rough wood pillar every ten feet. The establishment looked to be out of scale in this tiny village.

"Hello, Padre," Billy called out as we stepped into the dry goods store.

"Well, hello, Billy," Polaco walked from behind the counter with a big smile. "It is good to see you," he sounded like he meant it as the two shook hands.

"Padre, this is my good friend, Robert O'Dell," Billy continued with the formalities as Polaco and I shook hands. He was a short, stocky man who looked like he could break an axe handle in half.

"Yes, we met several months ago," Polaco put his hand on my shoulder. "When Mr. O'Dell and his wife were on their way to Sunnyside. He is in the very important position of postmaster there. How are you getting along in your new home?"

"It couldn't be any more agreeable," I explained. "Once we quit losing our chickens to the coyotes. We couldn't ask for a better arrangement."

"Go," Polaco pointed to a door to our right. "Have a seat in the cantina. I will get you a drink. It is a long ride from Fort Sumner. Tonight, you fellows are in business," he leaned toward us as though he was telling us a secret.

"Esmeralda, she has made some tamales. You will have a fine meal here," he said with a broad smile.

We went into the next room which had a twelve foot long bar and six tables. We sat facing the bar as Polaco filled two tall glasses of beer for us. "Would you prefer a glass of whiskey?" the big man smiled as he delivered the beer.

"No, thank you," Billy said.

I shook my head, "This is fine."

"It's so good to see you fellows," Polaco grinned as he stood over our table. "Let me go encourage Esmeralda to prepare a meal for you."

There were only two other people in the cantina. Standing near the center of the bar was an elderly Hispano man. He sipped his whiskey while he stared at the bottles behind the counter. In the corner, to our left, sat a pretty Mexican woman. She wore a white blouse and red skirt. Her shining black hair was adorned with a yellow flower. Now, I understood why Billy had cleaned himself up at the river.

We had just finished our beer when a short, wide hipped Mexican woman approached our table with a tray full of food. She seemed very happy as she set a plate with two tamales in front of each of us. She also had two bowls of pasole and two bowls of green chili. In the center of the table, she set a plate stacked with warm tortillas.

"Gracias," Billy offered his most endearing smile to Esmeralda.

"De nada," she said as she stared at him with a look she might give to her favorite nephew.

Esmeralda left and Polaco came in and stood over the table. "Well, this ought to fix you fellows up just fine," he smiled with approval.

"It might as well be Christmas," Billy said as he dipped a tortilla in the green chili.

"This is a fine meal, Padre," I agreed.

"Excuse me, please," Polaco left to deal with someone in the store.

"Why do we bother with forks and knives, Robert," Billy seemed to have something important on his mind. "You can accomplish everything there is about eating with a spoon."

To prove his point, he cut off a large piece of tamale with his spoon and stuffed it into his mouth. "Hee?"

I just shook my head. This kid's mind seemed to be going every direction at once. I hoped there wouldn't be too many more surprises, like the antelope chase, before we got the equipment back to Sunnyside.

We worked our way through most of the food

53

on the table. I had eaten all I could. Billy had finished his tamales and pasole. He was working his way through the stack of tortillas. He pointed at what was left of my green chili. I slid the bowl across to him.

At this time, a man walked through the door and went to the bar. He was wearing a black hat with the brim turned down. His Texas Marino spurs announced his entrance. He wore a red bandana and had a red sash tucked into his belt. I had seen several Texans pass through Sunnyside with a similar sash.

"Gimme some room," he said to the old man at the bar.

The viejo looked at him but did not move.

Next to me, I saw Billy's eyes narrow.

"I said move it, greaser," the Texan shoved the old man.

Billy stood up. He stepped to the left of the table. With his left hand, he pulled the red serape away from the gun on his right hip.

"Mister," he called out.

The Texan looked over his left shoulder.

"I'd say you're shy a few manners," Billy said as his right hand went down to his revolver.

"Sit down, Nancy," the Texan replied.

Billy's narrow jaw was pushed forward. "I say you owe my friend an apology." Billy's

54

fingers touched the handle of his gun.

"Sit down if you don't want trouble, sonny," the Texan seemed to be caught off guard.

"You apologize and we won't have no trouble," Billy's eyes did not blink.

"In about one minute, they're gonna carry you out of here feet first," the Texan said without much conviction.

"This conversation is finished, mister," Billy said with little emotion. "Apologize to my friend or get busy."

The Texan turned part way around. He seemed undecided.

Billy nodded, "It's your call."

The Texan studied Billy for a moment. Then he turned to the old man. "My apology, Senor." With that, he crossed the room and went out the door. Billy watched him leave. He moved his chair to the other side of the table so he could watch the door.

The old man left the bar and came to our table.

"Gracias, senor," he stared into Billy's face as he reached out his right hand.

"No es nada, mi amigo," Billy smiled as he stood to shake hands with him. The old man's eyes were watery as he stared at Billy. Billy nodded and patted the old man on the shoulder.

Billy looked satisfied as he sat down to finish his meal. It was as if he had just chased a mongrel dog out of the cantina. His exhibition of courage was somewhere between heroic and reckless. It was clear he liked to play to the crowd, even if the crowd was only myself and two strangers. He had no apparent concern for death. His or the Texan's.

"You'd better watch you back for a couple days," I suggested. I had grown up in a neighborhood full of Irish scrappers, but I had never seen anything like this.

"These dang tortillas are cold," Billy dismissed my concern. It seemed like his standoff with the Texan was already forgotten.

Padre Polaco came rushing in from the store. "What is all this?"

"Well," I said. "Billy just denied this fella from Texas a glass of whiskey."

Billy nodded. "He insulted our friend, there."

"You would shoot a man over such a thing?" Polaco could not believe what had just happened. "That man has been here for two days. He is on his way to the Arizona Territory. He looks like a pistolero. You had better take care, Billy. This man may look for revenge."

Billy looked bored as he nodded.

Esmeralda approached our table with a big

smile.

"Would you nice men want a piece of apple pie?"

"No, thank you," I declined.

"Si, mochas gracias," Billy smiled.

I could not figure this boy who had become my fast friend. A few minutes before, he had risked his life to settle a matter of poor manners. Now, he was excited about a piece of apple pie.

Esmeralda delivered the pie. She fondly patted Billy on the head and stared at his face. He smiled in return and touched her arm. Then, he fell to work on the pie.

"You see this piece of pie, Robert?" he said with his mouth full.

I nodded.

"This is how I see this thing in New Mexico. Let's say you cut this pie eight ways. A fella like Boss Catron would say, I'll take seven pieces of this pie and the rest of you can divide up the last sliver between you. That's what they've done to these Mexican families in the territory. They're stuck with that last sliver of pie."

"I couldn't have explained it any better," I agreed.

"If you're looking for an honest man with any kind of authority," Billy continued his speech on political corruption, "You might as well stay clear of Santa Fe. Or Lincoln, for that matter."

"That's probably true, Billy."

"You know it and I know it," Billy finished his point as he wolfed down the last of the pie.

Padre Polaco walked back into the room, "Let me buy you fellows another beer," he motioned for us to join him at the bar.

"Excuse me," Billy said. He headed over to the corner table where the pretty young woman had been batting her eyes at him.

I joined Polaco at the bar as he poured me a beer.

"So what's this business with the Texans with the red sashes?" I was curious to learn about the man that Billy had run out of the cantina in case we found him waiting for us on the road the next day.

"There is a man named Clanton who owns a big spread of land in Arizona, near the Mexican border. His vaqueros steal cattle from Mexico. Or he buys cattle from as far away as Utah or New Mexico. He pays pennies on the dollar. He has men who are experts in changing the brands. Brand artists, they call them.

"Clanton, he sells these cattle to mining camps all over the territory where there is a great need for beef. Or they are taken to John

Kinney in Mesilla who takes them to the panhandle in Texas. Other cattle, stolen from the Indian Reservation or John Chisum are taken back to Arizona.

"Clanton's ranch is nothing but a holding pen for stolen cattle. This business is very profitable for Clanton and Kinney, but the law is bringing pressure to close down this operation. So, Clanton brings in pistoleros from Texas or anywhere he can find them. That is why I worry about the incident with Billy. These are dangerous men."

"I only met the kid a few days ago," I confided as I looked over to the corner table where Billy and the Mexican girl were in a heart-felt conversation. "I've never met a more polite young fella. He's been on quite a journey since his mother died two years ago."

"It is very dangerous to try and settle these matters with a gun," Polaco warned. "Billy may be a fine boy, but he doesn't want to have men like these looking for him."

"I understand, Padre."

"I have a room in the next building where you can sleep. We have no hotel here, but this is a nice clean room for you and Billy."

"I appreciate you're generosity, Padre. I figure we can settle up in the morning."

I turned to collect Billy. He and the young woman were gone. I went outside to get my gear. Billy's grey mare was nowhere to be seen. I found the room and washed up. I stretched out on the comfortable bed and pondered the event in the cantina. I wondered what the future might have in store for this fearless boy. I fell asleep before I could pull my boots off.

4

I awoke at daybreak the next morning. I looked across the room at the other bed. No Billy. I washed up and collected my belongings. I went into to the empty cantina. Esmeralda hurried over to my table and poured me a cup of coffee.

"I make you breakfast," she smiled. "Where's Beely?"

"I don't know," I shrugged my shoulders.

"Tito," she called out. A boy of about seven came running into the cantina. "Ve busca a Beely."

"Beely?"

"Si, rapido."

The little boy ran out the door. I watched his small bare feet kick up dust as he raced across the plaza. A few minutes later, here came Tito. He burst into the cantina.

"Mama, Mama," Tito out of breath. "Lo Encontre!"

Esmeralda smiled at the little boy, "Gracias, mi hijo."

About the time Esmeralda brought me a plate of eggs and beans with tortillas and green chili, I saw Billy heading this way across the open square. He was tucking in his white shirt. He carried his threadbare red serape in the other hand. He tried to pull the serape over his head, but he had forgotten to take off his sombrero. The serape got tangled up with the hat.

He had to start over. Drop the hat and serape on the ground. Tuck in the shirt. Now, pull the serape over your head. Pick up the hat. Dust it off and fix it on your head. Now, he was ready to start the day.

He entered the cantina with that big toothy grin and sat down. "I was waiting for word from you," he explained. "To hear if you were ready to go."

"You were, huh?" I looked him over. I doubted that he had gotten any sleep.

"Oh, yeah," He nodded. "I've been ready since first light. Ready to travel."

"Well, that's good to know, Billy."

"This transport business ain't for late risers," he assured me.

"Well, you're just in time for breakfast. You get any sleep?"

"Oh, plenty of sleep," Billy nodded, but his eyes betrayed him. "Hortencia is a fine girl."

"I think she liked the way you stood up for the old man, yesterday."

"She told me that very thing. All night, in fact. That old man is her father. She claimed I made some good friends here at Puerto de Luna."

"You made some friends and you made Padre Polaco very nervous."

"Well," Billy said," I did what any man would do. You can't let a friend be disrespected in that manner."

"Had you met the old fellow when you came through here with Heiskell Jones?"

"That makes no difference," Billy admitted that he had never met the man. "I can't stand aside and allow that kind of an insult."

So there it was. Billy had decided to be the protector of the downtrodden with his quick revolver. While I admired his sense of honor, I thought it might prove to be a dangerous line of work.

We finished breakfast while Esmeralda stood

in the corner and smiled at Billy. He could barely keep his eyes open, but he cleaned up his meal in short order. This skinny kid could eat.

We went to get the wagon, which was already loaded with the postal equipment. I tied my horse to the back of the wagon. Billy threw his saddle and bridal into the wagon.

"Gracie will follow along side." Billy explained.

As we rolled through the plaza, I saw Hortencia standing next to a small adobe hut. I elbowed Billy and pointed in her direction. Billy took off his sombrero and held it against his chest. His smile was genuine. Hortencia smiled and waved. She had not had time to fix her hair. She looked like a girl with love on her mind.

We started south on the road to Sunnyside. It was another clear day. Gracie trotted along side Billy and watched his every move. I had seen dogs with this kind of attachment to a human, but never a horse.

A large herd of antelope grazed on the east side of the road. I looked over at Billy. He was too tired for another chase. He would start to fall asleep and catch himself when his head began to drop. A man couldn't sleep while he earned his pay as a freighter. I enjoyed the quiet as the two mules trotted south.

We stopped for lunch in a grove of cottonwoods with the Pecos gurgling along next to us. I expected to see the man from Texas at any time. Esmeralda had wrapped up four tamales along with two apples. After Billy wolfed down his food, he began to come to life again.

"You know, Robert, my best friend in Silver City was an old man named Elias Roybal. He was a rope maker by trade. He made the best lariats in the territory. I met him one day while I was wandering around the barrio, killing time. South of town, on a little hill, was the Mexican part of town. They called it 'Chihuahua'.

"I watched the old man for several hours as he made those fine lariats. He would sit in a chair and move the chair into the shade as the sun crossed the sky. Later, in the cold days of winter, he would keep the chair in the sun as he worked.

"The next day, I went back to watch Elias work and he had two chairs. We would move our chairs together as he worked and taught me to speak Spanish. If he needed something, I would fetch it and he didn't have to get out of his chair. It was a fine arrangement all the way around.

"For two years, I spent as much time as I could with Elias. I was like family. When he and Adela would eat, I would eat. I mostly learned Spanish over all that good cooking. They had two sons who had been killed after they resisted their land being stolen.

"The Roybal family had been granted eight hundred acres along the Rio Grande, south of Albuquerque. They had farmed and raised sheep on the land going back to his grandfather. When they were informed by the constable that their land now belonged to a lawyer in Santa Fe, his two sons refused to leave.

"One evening, on their way home, they were shot dead by a group of hired gun hands. There was no way to prove that these men were paid by the lawyer, so Elias and Adela moved south to the barrio in Silver City. The only selection these Mexican families had was to move into a town or take their sheep to poor grazing land not owned by these new ranches.

"Elias told me that's what's happened all over the territory. These Mexicans had no one to take their side in a courtroom. They had to abandon their homes and their land. All they could do is try to scratch out a living by any means they could. Boss Catron and his friends in Santa Fe have made themselves rich off of

66

these Mexican families. There's not much that can be done about it, but you don't have to like it."

"The people at the top always seem to win out, Billy," I agreed. "They make the laws. They have the cleverest lawyers. Money is power and they have the money."

Billy reached out and rubbed Gracie's neck, "Give me the Mexican people any day. They're the most honest folks I know in these parts. Elias and Adela are the finest people I ever met. While I watched Elias work, I used to think about his sons. One day this little verse came to me:

> *Oh timid Mexicans, don't be afraid,*
> *Listen to the sound of the bullets,*
> *The bullets of those gringos say:*
> *Chee chee cha ree,*
> *If you don't kill me,*
> *I shall kill thee.*

It was all starting to make sense to me. Other than his mother and maybe his brother, Billy had not experienced much kindness during his young life. He had no use for his stepfather, who was just another hard case. Elias Roybal was probably the closest thing to a father that he

67

had ever known. His fight was Billy's fight. Billy had made his decision to side with the dispossessed Hispanos. It was an honorable decision, but he had chosen the losing side.

"You know, Billy, you're not the only one who's spent some time in jail. When I was twenty-two, my younger brother, Danny, and I decided to make some easy money. We took up prize fighting. I guess we were inspired by the great Charlie Gallagher. It was illegal at the time. but there was a fight every Saturday night somewhere in Chicago.

"We trained for about a year with the help of an old fella named Battler Bill Donovan. We learned all the moves and holds. We beat each other's brains in on a regular basis. Danny was quicker, but I was bigger, so it evened out.

"Our first two fights were at Petryl's Saloon on West 19th Street, down on the South Side. Queensbury rules. Five-ounce gloves. We won our first two bouts and they started calling us 'the Daring O'Dells'. Hell, Billy, we figured we would never have to work again.

"So our third bout was across the Indiana state line in a place called Roby. It was nothing but a big barn on the edge of town. A promoter named O'Malley set it up.

"Danny and I both won. He fought

lightweight and I fought middleweight. Danny was a natural showman. He could work up the crowd like nobody else. He'd have his man ready to fall, but he'd let him go to extend the bout and keep the crowd all lathered up.

"Anyway, during the heavyweight bout, the local constables swarmed in and arrested all of us. There must have been thirty of them. Who knows how much money they confiscated. They arrested all the fighters, but O'Malley must have given them the slip.

"Danny and I spent three days in the Roby jail. It was August and it seemed like there was no air to breathe inside that cell. The food was mostly stale biscuits and beans. We didn't know if we would ever get out. One by one, the other fighters were bailed out, but not Danny and I.

"I suppose if we had sat there a few more days, we would have contacted my father, but we feared his lecture more than the judge. Of course, this would never have happened in Chicago. The cops would have gotten a piece of the gate. They also would have had action on all the fights.

"I suppose O'Malley finally bailed us out. Someone did. We never saw our purse money. That was it for me. I never wanted to sit in one of those jail cells again. I took a job as a reporter with the Chicago News and Mail. That's when I met Susan. When she had just started teaching school.

"I figure it's better to be an ex-prize fighter. An undefeated middleweight," I looked over at Billy. He nodded, seriously. He had listened to my story with keen interest.

"Maybe you can teach me to use my fists, Robert."

I ran my fingers over my broken nose and thought for a minute. With his quickness and lack of fear, Billy might have made a fine welterweight. I doubted that his delicate hands could have taken the abuse.

"I think you've already found your answer, Billy. On your hip, there."

"Maybe so," Billy nodded.

"Danny is still fighting up there. We've all tried to talk him into quitting the game. I don't think he even cares about the money. It's all the attention he gets around town. He can't go anywhere in Chicago without someone hollering, 'Danny O'Dell.' And, of course, the ladies all want to make his acquaintance."

As the day wore on, the sap began to rise in Billy. He started singing, "*And it's Brennan on the Moor, Brennan on the Moor, young, brave and undaunted was young Brennan on the*

70

Moor...."

I joined in on the second chorus and soon we were singing at the top of our lungs. Each of us was trying to sing louder than the other. We got to laughing so hard that we couldn't finish the song.

I pointed at him and tried to say, "Young Brennan, tis it?" I was laughing so hard the words would not come out. Billy shook his head, no. He knew what I was trying to say. He was laughing so hard he had tears in his eyes.

Billy was in better spirits after the song. He recounted practical jokes that he and his school chums used to play in Silver City. Harry and Wayne Whitehill, Chauncy Truesdell, Louis Abraham and the Bennet boys. The victim was usually the Chinaman who had set himself up for scorn after his decision about the Negro baby.

Billy said the editor of the local paper called them the "Street Arabs". After school, they would bet on each other in foot races. Harry Whitehill was easily the fastest. One afternoon, he and Billy decided to fix the race. Whitehill pretended to stumble. He and Billy collected the other boy's money. It was just for a laugh, Billy said.

He told me all about a young teacher who

had arrived in Silver City. Mary Richards had come from England and she had the most beautiful eyes Billy had ever seen. She spoke four languages, while Billy could only speak two. She could write with either hand and so could he. This convinced Billy that they must have been related somehow. He said that this was the year that he began to take his education seriously.

We finally rolled into Sunnyside about an hour after dark. Susan was happy to see us. She had made a roast with potatoes. We were tired from the trip. We washed up and enjoyed a fine meal. Afterwards, we sipped our tea and talked about Puerto de Luna. I left out the part about trouble in the cantina and Billy's night with Hortencia. I could fill in those details later.

We offered Billy a place to sleep in the main room, but he said he'd keep company with Gracie in the stable. Susan told him that a letter had come for him.

Billy was in a hurry to read the letter. "George Coe has offered me a job on his ranch. Down on the Ruidoso."

"There you go," I said.

"That's wonderful news, Billy," Susan agreed.

"When a friend asks for your help, the only

thing to do is go," Billy explained. In truth, he had no other options. "George and his cousin, Frank, are good men. They both play the fiddle. Along with Dick Brewer, Doc Spurlock and Charley Bowdre, they have ranches south of Lincoln."

"Sounds like a good bunch to get started with," I encouraged him.

"Once I get settled, I might look into my own piece of property down there," Billy stared at the letter. "Start off small."

"That's a fine idea," Susan agreed. "Put down some roots so you can put an end to this wandering."

"I have to find a place somewhere," Billy nodded.

Billy was excited as he went off to bed. The next morning, it was all we could do to make him wait for breakfast. He hurried through his meal, which was common, but he didn't say much, which was uncommon. As he stood up, he thanked us for being his friends and all the kindness.

He brought Gracie around from the stable and met us on the road. He climbed into the saddle and took off his hat.

"I hope to see you folks soon," Billy smiled down at us. "You and the Jones family are as close to kin as I have in these parts."

"We feel that way too, Billy," Susan smiled up at the boy.

"Well, I 'd better be kickin'," Billy pointed his horse south. "Adios," he said. With a wave of his sombrero, he and Gracie were off.

5

Three days after Billy left for the Ruidoso, another stranger rode into town. It was late afternoon. A big man on a tall Missouri mule stopped in front the post office. He wore a brown hat with the wide brim turned down. I went out to say hello.

"That a fine looking animal," I was impressed by size of the mule and the shine of his coat.

"Moses shows the way," the man's expression did not change. He might be considered handsome if one were partial to bushy eyebrows and a broad nose over a thick black mustache.

"Harold Early," he said as he dismounted. He reached out his large hand as he walked toward me. He was about six-foot-two. He had a confident ease about him.

"Robert O'Dell," I reached out to shake hands.

"The British Crown might consider this a conspiracy," he said with a straight face. "Two Irishmen idling in the street."

I laughed, "And I might be fortunate enough to own a pitchfork."

The big man chuckled, "That pitchfork would make you the best armed man in the brigade."

"Possibly officer material."

"At a minimum," Harold laughed.

"From what part of the country did the Earlys hale?

"Well, it was O'Loughrey at one time. Mulmoher before that. They left County Cork in '46, looking for that next potato."

"Come over to the house, Harold," I was immediately comfortable with the big Irishman. "We'll see if I can find something to for us to drink. You might as well stay for supper."

"I tell ya, Robert, the occasional sit down meal is the only thing that makes this line of work tolerable. I'm a reporter for the Daily Optic out of Las Vegas. My territory covers San Miguel, Lincoln and Dona Ana counties. I spend most of my days on the road."

"I take the papers from Las Vegas and Santa Fe. We're new out here."

"If you read those papers, there will be a lot that you will never know. Old man Hersh is the exception. He runs the only halfway honest newspaper in these parts. The others grovel at the feet of Boss Catron in Santa Fe."

We want into the small adobe house. I offered Harold a seat at the table.

"Susan, this is Harold Early. He's a reporter for the Las Vegas Optic. I thought if he stayed for supper, we might learn a thing of two."

"It's so nice to meet you, Harold," Susan stepped out of the kitchen. "I'll have some stew ready shortly, if you care to eat with us."

I could see that Harold was impressed with Susan as his face lit up with a big smile. "I couldn't be any happier if this was the finest restaurant in San Francisco," he flattered her.

"Shall we cut the dust with a glass of whiskey?" I reached for a bottle of Jameson's.

"I'd be a fool to decline," Harold laughed. "You don't often get a wee drop from the top shelf out here."

"My father-in-law keeps us in stock for these very occasions," I explained as I poured us each a glass. "He still has hopes of me running his tannery one day."

Harold took a sip and leaned back in his chair, "As they say, if it wasn't for good whiskey, the Irish would rule the world. I wouldn't be one to stand in the way of that lofty endeavor, but you're always going to need a good man to stay behind and guard the women and the whiskey."

"And who better than a man on a mule?"

"Precisely," Harold nodded.

"We made the acquaintance of another young Irishman here a few days ago. Goes by the name of William Bonney."

"I know the lad," Harold said as he tipped back his brown hat.

"You know Billy?" Susan called out from the kitchen.

"I met the boy down at Seven Rivers. He was staying with Heiskell and Maam Jones. They took him in with their other nine boys. Don't say anything unkind about Billy in the presence of Maam Jones."

"He's a curiosity, isn't he," I said.

"He put on a shooting and riding exhibition for us," Harold said. "That lad is quick as a cat and can shoot like nobody you've ever seen. He loves to play to the crowd."

"He came up here looking for work with

Pete Maxwell," I explained. "He had come across the southern part of the territory to get work with John Chisum, but what rancher is going to take that skinny kid seriously?"

"He's got his admirers down at Seven Rivers, I tell ya. All anybody talked about was Billy this and Billy that. He is a curiosity. His good manners and his friendly ways make you want to like the boy right off.

"It doesn't surprise me that Maxwell wouldn't hire him. He's an aristocrat here on the Pecos. Inherited the town and all the land as far as the eye can see from his father. Lucian Maxwell. When the father bought the fort and the surrounding land from the government for five thousand dollars, he brought twenty-five or thirty families with him from the Cimarron. Pete employs mostly Mexican vaqueros whose fealty he can rely on."

"We took a short trip to Puerto de Luna, Billy and I. To pick up some equipment for the post office. While we are having supper in Padre Polaco's cantina, this Texan comes in for a drink.

"There was an elderly Hispano at the bar. This Texan tells him to give him some room, but the old man didn't seem to understand. So the Texan gives him a shove and calls him a greaser.

"Next thing I know, Billy stands up and tells the Texan that he has poor manners. Billy tells him to apologize to the old man or they'll settle things right there. At first, the Texan didn't take the kid seriously.

"So Billy repeats that either the Texan apologizes or goes to work with his gun. The Texan took stock of the situation for a moment. Then apologized and left. It was the damnedest thing you ever saw. Next thing I know, Billy disappears with this pretty Mexican girl."

"There's a lad with a future," Harold smiled. "They told me he wandered into Seven Rivers nearly dead after some scrape with the Apaches. They said his feet were so bloody that they had to cut the boots off of him.   From what I saw, he's a natural born talker who gets on with everybody."

"Billy was all business in that cantina," I explained.   "You see that sort of slander against Hispanos fairly often around here, but Billy was going to make that Texan pay the ultimate price for insulting that old man."

"Maybe somebody whaled the tar out of him as a kid," Harold offered. "It happens that way sometimes. When a kid takes too many hidings, he comes out the other end with a sharp temper.

"While I was in Seven Rivers, the Widow Casey came through with her two boys and a small herd of cattle. Billy offered to see them safe to Texas, but Mrs. Casey was reluctant to travel with the young stranger. From what you're telling me, she might have been wise to take him along.

"Robert Casey had run a small ranch down on the Hondo. He was well regarded by everyone. He would have been a welcome guest at this table. Very entertaining fellow. Three years ago, he was killed by a rip named William Wilson. Wilson was caught and sentenced to hang. I am expected to witness such events in my line of work.

"So they stretch Wilson and let him dangle for about five minutes. They bring him down and toss him into a pine box. A few minutes later, a commotion is heard inside the coffin. They open the lid and discover that Wilson is still among the living. So what do they do?

"The authorities talk over the matter and decide that Wilson will have to be rehanged. That's when I took my leave. They pay me to report on a hanging, but I don't see any extra wages if the poor devil is hanged a second time.

"Anyway, Casey's widow had lost her land when a lawyer, named McSween, discovers through court records that the Caseys had never filed a proper claim on the land even though they had worked the property for years. A young Englishman, named Tunstall, ended up with the land. So the Widow Casey stole back her own cattle and was on her way to Texas."

Susan put three plates on the table and went back to get the pot of stew. She dished up our food and laid out a plate of biscuits. All Harold could do was smile at her.

"You know anything about a character named Jesse Evans?" I was curious to learn about the cattle thief that Billy had mentioned.

"Pure Killer," Harold said as he finished a mouthful of stew. "He and John Kinney have been shooting up Dona Anna County for some time now. On New Years Eve, three years ago, Kinney goes into this saloon in Las Cruces. He gets into a row with a soldier and takes the short end of the scuffle.

"Kinney goes out and collects Evans and a few others. They kick open the door of the saloon and commence to shooting. Two soldiers were killed and two were wounded. One civilian was also killed. Is Kinney brought up on charges? Not a chance. Sheriff Barela is in league with Kinney. By turning his head, he gets a share of the proceeds from the stolen livestock."

I thought I would give Harold time to finish his stew while he smiled at my wife. He was a big man with a big appetite. Susan was always happy to feed a stranger, but I had the notion that we might see more of Harold.

"The Mes Gang were Kinney's primary rivals in stealing cattle in Dona Ana," Harold continued his story. "Kinney and Evans didn't favor their interference so they laid in wait and killed four members of the Mes Gang. Since the dead men were Mexicans, no charges were brought up.

"A few weeks later, Evans kills a man named Fletcher in broad daylight in Las Cruces. While all this is going on, Governor Axtell appoints William Rynerson as district attorney for Dona Ana, Lincoln and Grant counties.

"Axtell is a creation of Thomas Catron in Santa Fe. Rynerson is a confederate of John Kinney's as well as Jimmy Dolan. In fact, Rynerson loaned Dolan the money to throw in with Lawrence Murphy in Lincoln. Let's just say, any prosecution of Jesse Evans will be less than full throated.

"Knowing that he has friends in high places, a few months later, Evans and his boys kill three more Mexicans at Shedd's Ranch. This was a collection point for stolen livestock moving from New Mexico to Arizona or Texas. It's similar to Ike Clanton's operation in Arizona. Why raise beef if you can buy stolen cattle for pennies on the dollar. No arm of the law will go near Shedd's Ranch."

Harold mopped up the last of the gravy on his plate with a biscuit. He would look up long enough to smile and then go back to work with his biscuit. Susan poured us more tea and we waited for Harold to continue.

"When Lawrence Murphy and his partner, Emile Fritz, got thrown out of their sutlers store at Fort Stanton in '73 for bilking the Army and the Mescalero Reservation, do they lose their beef contracts with the government? No, indeed. They merely pack up and move their operation to Lincoln.

"Here was the swindle that Murphy employed at the fort. He would keep three fat steers at his ranch near Carrizozo. He would buy stolen cattle from Mexico for next to nothing. These dobies were undersized and of very poor quality.

"So Murphy gets a contract to bring, say, two thousand head of cattle to the fort. He brings up these scrawny dobies along with his three fat steers. The officer in charge of the inspection has been gambling away his wages in Murphy's saloon and is probably in debt to Murphy. So the three fat steers are weighed to determine an average weight for the entire herd. The compromised officer then signs off on the deal.

"Is Murphy content with this larceny? No, he's not. At night, he sends out a handful of cowhands wearing Indian moccasins. They wave blankets and drive the cows out of the holding pen. By morning, the cows have scattered in all directions. The Indians are blamed and the cattle are later rounded up and taken back to Murphy's ranch. It was called the miracle herd. It never got any smaller.

"Murphy used a similar ploy with at least one wood contract. He had his men stack the wood in squares with a hollow center to drive up the count. Then, for good measure, one of his boys sneaks in at night and starts a fire in the wood yard.

"Murphy's lust for theft knew no boundaries. When Murphy was finally exposed, he was run out of Fort Stanton with no more than a verbal dressing down. He had no fear of prosecution. His good friend, Tom Catron, was the U.S. Attorney for New Mexico Territory.

"If Murphy's crooked operation at Fort Stanton was lucrative, the right kind of operation in Lincoln could be a bonanza that would control commerce in the whole county. The problem is that Murphy needs financing. Just because he's been swindling the government doesn't mean he has anything to show for it. So, who does he turn to? Why, Thomas Catron's First National Bank in Santa Fe. Catron's not about to turn his back on an opportunity to fleece the good people of Lincoln County and maintain the government beef contracts.

"Now, Murphy's partner, Fritz, is feeling a might sickly, so he decides to go back to die in Germany. Understand, Murphy is a man with no money, but he has a great talent for larceny. So, Catron pulls a few strings and gets Murphy appointed as probate judge in Lincoln. With his sterling record, why not? A few months later, when twenty thousand dollars in tax revenue goes missing, Murphy is forced to step down. You might say, he got in, made his move, then was himself removed.

"With Fritz on his way to Germany and the tax revenue thievery having dried up, Murphy needs a new partner. He's been handed a sure deal, but can he steal enough to make a go of it? Well, up steps Jimmy Dolan from Mesilla to partner up with Murphy. Now Dolan doesn't have a red cent either, but he is financed by none other than Catron's good friend, William Rynerson, the new D.A.

"The two impoverished partners put all their funding into building a two story mercantile in Lincoln. 'The House', they call it. The problem is they've run out of money for inventory, so they stock their store on credit from an outfit in St. Louis called, Spiegelberg Bros.

"Murphy and Dolan soak up the whiskey with the best of them and they've never run onto a crooked scheme that they won't embrace, but they are completely inept businessmen. Because they have to service so much interest on three loans, they have to skin the local folks by overcharging for everything. The citizens of Lincoln are not at all happy with this arrangement.

"So, a year ago, in steps John Tunstall. He's a young Englishman whose father has more money than God. He builds a first rate dry goods store across the street from Murphy and Dolan. Tunstall is also encouraged by lawyer McSween to buy up four thousand acres of grazing land south of Lincoln, mostly on the Rio Feliz. He intends to compete for beef contracts with the Army and the Mescalero Reservation.

"Comfortably sipping whiskey from a silver flask, in the security of his South Springs Ranch,

John Chisum is encouraging the two newcomers to engage in an all out battle against Murphy and Dolan. Chisum had sold his ranch on the Bosque Grande to an outfit from St Louis and started another operation near Roswell. The capper is that Chisum, Tunstall and McSween have started a bank in Lincoln. This can't sit well with Catron in Santa Fe.

"Understand that Murphy is an old man in failing health, but Dolan is a mean little weasel who won't stand for any infringement on his new found empire. Mark my words, there will be bloodshed south of here. And the law is all lined up on the side of Murphy and Dolan."

"When Dolan left Mesilla for Lincoln, he brought Jesse Evans and his band of killers with him." Harold counted off his fingers, "Pony Diell, George Spawn, Jim McDaniels, Frank Baker, George Davis, Tom Hill, Nicholas Provencio, Bob Martin, Bill Allen, Manuel Segovia, Billy Morton, Sarafin Aragon, Roscoe Burrell, Ponciano Domingues, Bob Nelson. I think I got all of them. If there is an honorable man in the bunch, I haven't met him.

"Dolan will also have the support of the Seven Rivers Warriors, as they call themselves. The Jones boys, who are Billy's friends. The Beckwith brothers. The Olinger brothers, who are strictly low grade ore. Marion Turner, Milo Pierce, Andy Boyle, Lewis Paxton, and Buck Powell.

"This is mostly a group of small ranchers on the south Pecos who have resisted Chisum swallowing up hundreds of square miles of land where these folks would like to graze their cattle. For this reason, they feel justified in poaching Chisum's cows. Chisum won't take the losses sitting down, so he hires some gun hands from Texas. The old man is tired of seeing his stolen beeves sold at a discount to the government.

"That's the sum of it. You have Tunstall, McSween and Chisum aligned with some small ranchers south of Lincoln such as Dick Brewer, George and Frank Coe, Charlie Bowdre and Doc Spurlock. A handful of honest ranchers up against the most powerful outfits in the territory who have the backing of Catron in Santa Fe along with his hand picked lawmen and judges.

"If I were a gambling man, which I am, and I had to put up my last fifty dollars, which I don't have and don't expect to have any time soon, on one side, it would be the side that Catron is on. That's all you need to know about the fight that's about to take place south of here."

Harold slowly pushed his clean plate away

from him. "Mrs. O'Dell, that was the finest supper I've enjoyed in recent memory."

"How about a piece of pie," Susan asked.

"I'd be a fool to decline, Maam," Harold settled back in his chair.

"I'll make another pot of tea," she called over her shoulder.

I thought I saw Harold shoot a glance at the shelf where I kept the whiskey, but I could have been mistaken.

"How did you folks end up out here at the crossroads?" Harold called into the kitchen.

"I thought I had a teaching position in Santa Fe," Susan said as she set the pot of tea on the table. "It didn't work out. We were fortunate to be offered this opportunity at Sunnyside."

"So you're a school teacher," Harold beamed across the table. "That explains you're flawless enunciation." This was clearly a man who liked to flatter women. And lay it on thick.

"You are much too kind," Susan stared at the man who was full of compliments as well as beef stew. She could spot this sort of blarney at a distance, but it didn't mean she was opposed to the kind words. I figured that this was an Irishman with just enough education to be dangerous.

"Well," Harold said as he stared at the

ceiling, "I usually get through here about every six weeks, but I may have to reconfigure my schedule after that meal. This old army outpost should be good for a story or two."

'You're always welcome, Harold," Susan smiled. I could see that her resistance to Harold's line of malarkey had begun to weaken.

"We've learned more in the last half hour than I could ever have picked up from the newspapers," I agreed. "Our door is always open to an O'Loughrey."

Harold laughed. "Other than the Optic, you'll only learn the version of events that's supported by the Ring in Santa Fe. Catron's got all the money behind him. He demands loyalty from these cowardly editors.

"Where did you get your education, Harold?" It was Susan's favorite question.

"I attended two years at Kentucky University," Harold paused with his fork above the pie. I s'pose I'll always be a southern boy. My father opposed the notion of slavery, but his brother, Jubil, was busy burning down towns on his way to Washington. He darn near made it, but it put our family in an odd circumstance. We supported the Confederacy, but we couldn't support the idea of selling folks like livestock."

"General Early is your uncle?" I was

surprised.

"I've never met him. He was a tobacco farmer and lawyer in Virginia before the war. I hear that he's the most sociable man you would ever meet until he mounts his horse and starts waving that sabre," Harold laughed. "I don't claim to be kin anywhere north of the Mason-Dixon. Or at any army outpost, for that matter. Down South, I'd likely be the object of fond regard."

"We'd better give Moses a good feed," I suggested. "You can throw your bedroll in front of the fire if you like."

Harold struggled to his feet. I suppose, the stew and apple pie and the warmth of the fire had made him sleepy. When we crossed the road to the stable, he pulled a flask of whiskey out of his war sack.

"Another drop will do no harm," he said as he uncapped the flask and handed it to me.

"Here's to the O'Loughreys," I said and took a short swig.

"To the O'Loughreys," Harold repeated as he tipped the flask and drained a good portion of its contents. "Wherever the hell they may be."

I laughed and took another drink.

"You're a fortunate man, Robert," Harold appeared dead serious. "I haven't met Susan's equal in my six years traveling these parts. They broke the mold after her."

"I tell myself that very thing every day. This may not seem a likely place for folks like us to settle, but it got us away from those stockyards in Chicago."

"Chicago?" Harold stared at me.

"Her father owned a successful tannery near the Union Stockyards. He was determined that I should finish out my life scraping hides."

"My daddy was a farmer." Harold gazed across the stable. "Corn and sorghum, mostly. When I hired on with the Optic and learned that I could scratch out a living talking with folks and writing stories, the notion of farming began to seem like a thankless task."

"What are the odds," I said. "I scrambled around chasing stories for the Chicago News and Mail for almost five years to avoid that tannery."

"Well," Harold smiled as he took another swallow, "Dodging work does not make us any less Irish."

We got Moses fed and went back to the house. Harold tossed his bedroll on the floor and stretched out. I had no sooner closed the bedroom door and started to pull my boots off when it sounded like the railhead had reached

Sunnyside. The plank floor shook every time the big man inhaled. Susan and I listened in disbelief as that locomotive ran all night.

6

As fall turned to winter, there were few travelers on the road. A snowstorm would delay the stage for as much as a week. The nights were cold, but nothing like Chicago. The days were clear and comfortable. In the evening, we were an old married couple, sitting by the fire. Susan liked to read novels while I concentrated on the three papers from Santa Fe and Las Vegas.

The early nightfall and the cold were not without reward. We would throw a log on the fire and repair to the bedroom. Susan would light a candle and take her light red hair down. I would watch from bed as she brushed out the curls. This could last twenty minutes. She was well aware of my anticipation as I waited. I would study her narrow waist and rounded hips in the flickering light. Finally, she would change into her nightgown and climb into bed.

In mid-November, the was a piece in the Santa Fe New Mexican that announced the opening of John Tunstall's new store in Lincoln. The mercantile was across the street from Lawrence Murphy's store. The article described Tunstall's store as a "fortress like, one story building with iron bars on the windows and an area set aside for a bank." Alexander McSween and John Chisum were given as Tunstall's partners in the bank. The article reported that the new venture would compete with Murphy for dry goods sales as well as beef contracts.

There was another short piece in the Gazette about John Kinney killing a man named Ysabel Barella. Kinney and his gang had then fled to Silver City in Grant County.

The same week, the Las Vegas Daily Optic had a story about a confrontation between Lincoln County Sheriff William Brady and John Tunstall. Brady had been drinking when he walked into Tunstall's store and called him a fool to challenge "The House." The sheriff promised Tunstall that he would not have a very long run in Lincoln. An argument ensued and Brady pulled his revolver. The situation was defused when Alexander McSween convinced

Brady that he could not shoot an unarmed man.

A week later, the Optic carried a story about Jesse Evans and three other members of his gang being broken out of jail in Lincoln by a gang of men from the Seven Rivers area. Being short of mounts, the gang stole eight horses from John Tunstall.

In late November, a letter from Billy arrived. Susan was all smiles as she read it to me:

Dear Robert and Susan,

Everything is going fine here on the Ruidoso. George and I snowed in for three days. Nothing to do but tell lies and stoke the fire. On Saturdays, George and Frank get out their fiddles and we sing songs and dance with the local gals. Wish you were here to enjoy our bailes.

With fond regards, Billy

With a foot of snow on the ground, Susan and I were spending most of our time in our small adobe home. With the plank floor and a good fireplace, we were comfortable, but spring could not arrive soon enough. Susan was getting restless. She decided that she would try

97

to set up a classroom at Fort Sumner when the weather cleared. I encouraged the idea as she was becoming somewhat irritable at this lonely outpost.

I concentrated on my newspapers. I tried to square the news with the background information that Harold Early had given us. I figured we would see the tall Kentuckian sometime before Christmas.

In early December, a story appeared in the Santa Fe paper that indicated that District Attorney William Rynerson, the same man who had bankrolled Jimmy Dolan to form a partnership with Lawrence Murphy, had filed charges against attorney Alexander McSween. The charge was embezzlement of insurance money owed to Murphy.

As a partner of Tunstall's, the article continued, Tunstall's property as well as McSween's assets would be attached until the matter was settled in court. It appeared that Catron and Murphy were going to use a legal maneuver to drive their competitors out of Lincoln County.

In late December, a second letter from Billy arrived. Susan read it and said, "Our young friend is full of hope."

The letter read:

Dear Robert and Susan,

Prospects here are much improved. I have hired on with an Englishman by the name of John Tunstall. He has bought thousands of acres south of Lincoln. He has also opened a store in town and he and McSween have opened a bank.

The days of Murphy and Dolan cheating folks around here are about ended. John is a highly educated man and treats everyone in a polite manner. He says I will some day manage one of his ranches. Short of that, Fred Waite and I are looking for a piece of land on the Rio Penasco where we can start our own operation.

Hope this piece of good news finds you both well. My best wishes at Christmas.

With regards, Billy

"I hope Harold is mistaken about a fight breaking out down there," I offered when Susan had finished the letter. "Billy can handle himself in a tight spot, but he'll be up against

99

some long odds."

"Harold also said that Murphy and Dolan were nearly broke," Susan reminded me. "Maybe, if they fail, Tunstall will become the driving force in the county and Billy will become his right hand man."

I doubted her optimism, "The problem is that Catron holds all the cards down there. The sheriff and the district attorney are in his hip pocket and his bank owns all of Murphy's assets. Then you have Rynerson who's heavily invested in the House. I wouldn't want to be in Tunstall's position with all the law backing the other side."

"Let's hope that Billy can stay out of the whole mess until it's all settled."

"Let's hope that crow doesn't find him."

"Why would you bring that up?" Susan scolded me. When she got angry, her lightly freckled cheeks would get flush. She never looked more beautiful.

"I shouldn't have. The trouble is that Billy can't seem to get that picture of the crow out of his head and neither can I. He's up against a group of seasoned killers down there. You know Murphy and Dolan won't go under without a fight."

"This is the first good news that that boy has gotten since his mother died." It was clear that

Susan's feelings for the boy ran deep. "He's been drifting about in the company of thieves and gamblers with no family and no prospects for a decent life. Now he has a chance to prosper with John Tunstall. Or he and his friend can find a place of their own."

"I'd like to see Billy start his own operation with this Waite fella. Stay clear of the fight between Tunstall and Murphy. Left on his own, there isn't anyone who that kid can't get along with."

I regretted that I had dampened Susan's optimism. There was no way to know what might happen in Lincoln. I reached for Susan's arm and pulled her against me. I wanted to kiss her while her cheeks were still flush.

7

A light snow was falling on the afternoon of Christmas Eve. I closed the post office and walked across the road to our small adobe home. Susan had a ham in the oven. The warmth from the corner fireplace along with the aroma of supper cooking made this seem like the finest place on the prairie.

I gave Susan my best Christmas Eve kiss and settled into the rocking chair by the fire. I was almost asleep when I heard a light knock from outside. When I opened the door, there was a tall man in a brown hat. Ice had collected in his mustache and his thick eyebrows.

"Hello, ya little Mick," he grinned.

"It's our wandering reporter," I said. "C'mon in and get those eyebrows thawed out."

"I'd better take care of Moses first. It's been a long journey from Lincoln. If I get near that fire, I'll never be able to get up."

"Hello, Harold." Susan walked toward the door with a big smile. "Now, it feels like Christmas."

"That very kind, Maam. I pushed Moses pretty hard to get here."

"We're so glad you're here." Susan had a genuine fondness for the man from Kentucky. "You can rest until supper."

I pulled on my coat and we walked out into the winter storm. There is no quiet like you feel during a falling snow.

We took Moses across the road to the stable. Harold unsaddled the mule while I grabbed some hay and a nosebag of oats. I could see why some men preferred to ride a mule. Besides having a reputation for being sure footed, this was the most peaceful animal I had ever seen.

"Moses thanks you for the oats."

"It's Christmas."

"Speaking of which," Harold said as he pulled a bottle of Jameson's out of his bedroll. "This set me back a few days pay, but nothing but the best for my Irish friend."

Harold broke the seal and handed the bottle

103

to me.

"To the folks in Chicago," I said and took a long pull of the fine whiskey.

"To the folks in Kentucky," Harold took a drink. "You know, Robert, I was set to spend Christmas in Lincoln. There are several good watering holes in town. I've been known to imbibe at the Wortley or the Patron House. Yesterday, I got to thinking about the folks back home. I got to feeling so lonesome for Kentucky that I had to get out of there. As rare as it may sound, you and Susan are as close to family as I have out here."

I took another swallow of whiskey. "Susan's feeling low about being so far from her family at this time of year. I'm glad you showed up. You might help to get her mind off Chicago."

"I'll do my level best," Harold nodded. "You know me. If I can help keep your wife happy, consider me duty bound."

We went back to the house. Harold took off his wet coat and hat and fell into the rocking chair by the fire. "If this ain't home."

I got two glasses from the kitchen. I took a seat on the other side of the fire and we had a bit more of the good whiskey.

"You missing Chicago?" Harold called to Susan.

"I am, indeed. We've never been this far from home at Christmas."

Harold stared at the fire. "All day, I've been thinking about my mother and pa. This was always a happy time on the farm. Mother would bake bread and pies. We'd trim out a goose and fill it with nuts and corn. We'd sit around and tell stories until it was time for supper."

"A goose is difficult to come by out here."

"This could be the finest restaurant in New York, as far as I'm concerned," Harold leaned back and closed his eyes.

"You always have the nicest things to say," Susan sounded happy. "You're a fine southern gentleman."

Harold laughed himself awake. "I spend most of my days in jail houses and saloons. Or some dusty sheep camp. I travel on the back of a Missouri mule. Are those your qualifications?"

"We meet a lot of folks out here at the crossroads," Susan began to set the table. "Not many of them are well spoken," Susan gave Harold a mild scolding. "Very few are well informed and none are as full of good humor."

"I stand corrected, Maam," Harold grinned. "I am a fine southern gentleman. It would clearly take a fool to think otherwise."

As we ate dinner, I could see that Harold was fading from his long ride in the snow. He made it through the ham and beans and summoned his last bit of reserve to finish the peach pie. I suggested that Harold throw his bedroll by the fire and we would call it a night. We could continue our discussion over breakfast in the morning.

The bright light coming through the frosted window at dawn told me the storm had ended and the sun was out. We all washed up and sat down to a fine breakfast of eggs with bacon and pinto beans along with tortillas and red chili. Harold looked more alert after a good night's sleep.

"We got a letter from Billy," Susan said. "Two letters, in fact. I think that lonely boy sees us as family, which is fine by us. He says he's gone to work for John Tunstall and Tunstall has promised him a future in his ranching business."

Harold thought for a moment. "Tunstall has hired a number of small ranchers south of Lincoln to form a bulwark against Murphy and his band of hired gunmen," Harold explained as he mopped around the edge of his plate with a warm tortilla. "They're a cut above the others who are fighting for control in Lincoln County.

"Dick Brewer has a good sized ranch of his

own. The Coes are forward thinking men who've planted an apple orchard and brought in the first hay-cutting machine. Billy's new best pal is a fella named Fred Waite, who has a college education form some outfit in St Louis.

"The problem is they are greatly outnumbered by a criminal bunch who will kill at the drop of a hat. They have corrupt judges and lawmen on their side, not to mention a crooked district attorney. Those are tall odds."

"You're certain that Billy has joined the wrong side of the fray," I asked.

"I think Tunstall has made a lot of promises to try and protect his new found interests," Harold continued. "If he wasn't in such a hurry to put Murphy and Dolan out of business, those two-bit crooks would accomplish that outcome on their own. Those whiskey soaks are up to their eyeballs in debt and to make matters worse, they extend credit to all their cronies who will never make good on it."

"You think Tunstall really has plans for Billy," Susan asked.

"Everybody likes Billy. You don't have to be around him for long to knows he's real sharp. He loves to be the center of attention and make folks laugh, but I fear that the wealthy Englishman is mostly interested in Billy's ability to handle a gun. George Coe told me that Billy is not only one of the best shots he's ever witnessed, but he's very quick."

It occurred to me that the Texan at Puerto de Luna had made a wise choice when he walked out of Padre Polaco's cantina. "There's no way Billy can stay out of the middle of this thing?"

"Not if he works for Tunstall. Jesse Evans tried to talk Billy into joining the other side. Murphy was willing to pay him good wages as a gun hand, but Billy turned him down. He seems to be fond of the Coes and Dick Brewer. It appears that he and the Englishman are thick as thieves. These fellas are determined to establish their own ranches and carve out a living."

"Are you going to spend Christmas with us," Susan asked as she filled our coffee cups.

"As much as I'd like to, I have to get back to Las Vegas," Harold leaned back with a contented look. "There's a year end bonus waiting for me at the Optic. We're all going to sit down and decide how to cover this impending mess in Lincoln."

"Well, if you have to go, you picked a good day to travel," I said.

"Moses and I have seen it all the past six years," Harold explained. "We'll make it to Padre Polaco's by nightfall. That cantina is a joyful spot in the middle of nowhere. The good Padre treats me as a friend."

"He's the most generous merchant I've ever dealt with," I agreed. "He didn't want to charge us for our meals or the room we stayed in. Rather, I stayed in. Billy arranged his own accommodations."

"Don't worry about ol' Polaco. He has a sizable herd of horses as well as cattle. He's the only game in town."

"We'll look forward to your next visit," Susan assured the big man.

"Don't get me wrong, Maam. This is my favorite place to stop all the way up the Pecos. You and Robert are the closest friends I have in these parts, although I'd understand if that comment made you a bit fearful," Harold grinned.

"Don't be foolish," Susan corrected him. "You and Billy are the best friends we've made in the six months we've been out here. I'm not sure which of you is more entertaining," She smiled.

Harold laughed, "Foolish would describe most of my decisions since I left Kentucky. I figure it's a compliment to be included in the same conversation with that little whirlwind. If the Irish don't stay together, there's little hope for any of us. Murphy and Dolan are probably telling each other that very same thing. The difference is that they're already stumbling drunk by this time of day."

Harold and I went to saddle Moses. Being it was Christmas, we had another nip of the belly warmer before he rode out onto the road. Susan walked out to meet us.

"Don't stay away too long," she looked up at Harold.

"I thank you for your kindness," Harold tipped his hat. "I'd better get moving. Luisa will be expecting me. That bonus money won't hurt my prospects any."

With a wave of his right hand, Harold headed north up the road. We stood shin deep in new snow and watched the tall mule trot out of sight. I wondered how long it would be before we heard about the opening salvo from Lincoln.

8

A week after Harold left, a surprising article appeared in the Las Vegas Gazette. It explained that Alexander McSween and his wife, along with John Chisum, had been arrested and taken to jail in Las Vegas. The charge against McSween was embezzlement of Emile Fritz's life insurance payoff. Chisum was a partner in the bank and, therefore, he was considered an accomplice in the scheme. Chisum was also charged with tax avoidance by refusing to declare the assets of his cattle holdings.

It appeared that McSween would be taken to Mesilla for arraignment. Chisum elected not to post bond. He would remain in jail. The embezzlement charge against McSween was silly on the face of it. Little remained of the

Emile Fritz life insurance payout. After the legal wrangling, the remainder would go to the Fritz family and not to Lawrence Murphy. This looked more like a ploy by Thomas Catron to bind Tunstall and Chisum to McSween and attach the property of all three.

I wondered if John Chisum's decision to remain in jail in Las Vegas might have something to do with his wanting to distance himself from any violence that might occur in Lincoln County. He would be out of danger in Las Vegas. Let Murphy and Tunstall go to war. Then, when the dust settled, he could move in and pick up the beef contracts.

There was a piece in the Daily Optic about a warrant being issued for Jesse Evans for theft of government mules from the Mescalero Apache Reservation. From what we had heard from Harold, stealing livestock from the Indian reservation was a centerpiece of the local economy.

The following week, The Santa Fe New Mexican reported that Lawrence Murphy and the House in Lincoln had mortgaged all of its assets to the First National Bank of Santa Fe, owned by Thomas Catron and partners. It appeared that it would now be Tunstall and McSween competing with Boss Catron for commerce in Lincoln County.

In early February, the Optic carried a story about Alexander McSween's preliminary hearing in Mesilla. District Judge Warren Bristol was too ill to conduct the hearing in court so the procedure was moved to Bristol's home. William Rynerson, who bankrolled Jimmy Dolan's failed partnership with Lawrence Murphy, acted as prosecutor. According to the article, which was likely written by Harold Early, Bristol and Rynerson missed no opportunity to insult McSween.

There was another curious note to the hearing. Judge Bristol, District Attorney Rynerson and Jimmy Dolan said that McSween had testified that he was a partner with John Tunstall in the store in Lincoln as well as his Rio Feliz ranch. After the hearing, McSween denied that he had said he was a partner with Tunstall. Deputy U. S. Marshall, Adolf Barrier, who attended the hearing and had no dog in the fight, said that McSween had never testified that he was a partner with Tunstall in the store or the ranch.

Judge Bristol declared that due to a lack of evidence on both sides, the matter would be postponed. This allowed the court to continue to attach the property of Tunstall and McSween. I

113

realized at this point that it was nearly impossible to expect legal remedies in New Mexico Territory where judges, prosecutors and law enforcement answered to one man in Santa Fe.

When the stage arrived the following Friday, I was anxious to see what had developed in Lincoln. McSween and Tunstall had arrived in town under the protection of Deputy Barrier. Tunstall found that Sheriff William Brady had already attached his store and his men were helping themselves to anything they favored.

McSween's large adobe house had also been attached. Sheriff Brady was set to arrest McSween and lock him up in the underground dungeon that served as a jail in Lincoln. Deputy Marshall Barrier was worried that McSween would be killed while in custody. In another show of courage, Barrier decided that he would keep Alexander McSween under house arrest in the McSween home.

All that was left for the Catron plan to be in full effect was for Sheriff Brady is to attach John Tunstall's Rio Feliz ranch as well as his livestock. I imagined that Tunstall must have felt that he was in a hopeless position with no legal recourse.

When the southbound stage delivered the

following weeks papers, the headline in the Santa Fe New Mexican made my jaw drop. JOHN TUNSTALL DEAD. The piece explained that Tunstall had resisted Sheriff Brady's posse when they attempted to attach a herd of horses that Tunstall and four of his men were taking from his Rio Feliz ranch to Lincoln. Shooting had ensued and Tunstall had been shot off his horse.

The story reported that Dick Brewer, John Middleton, William Bonney and Rob Widenmann had accompanied Tunstall, but they were ahead of the herd. When the shooting ensued, the four men fled for cover from the posse, which was estimated at forty-five men. The posse was under the direction of Deputy Sheriff Billy Mathews, who was also an employee of the House in Lincoln.

The New Mexican stated that an inquiry into the matter would be held. Until then, the killing of Tunstall was deemed justified in terms of the posse carrying out its sworn duty.

I sat back and considered the implications of this news. With the death of Tunstall, any future Billy might have had in Lincoln County had ended. Knowing the methods of the group that he was up against, he would be foolish to remain in the area. The decision would not be so easy for some of Tunstall's allies. They owned ranches and would not be inclined to leave.

The Las Vegas Gazette had a slightly different account of the Englishman's death. It said that Tunstall was taking his herd of horses to Lincoln to turn over to Sheriff Brady and allow the legal process to play out. The story reported that when a posse of forty-five men approached Tunstall's party, Tunstall's men fled for cover while Tunstall decided to ride back to explain that he was taking the horses to Lincoln to turn over to Sheriff Brady.

Tunstall was then shot off his horse in what was termed an overreaction by Brady's men. They then seized the herd of horses and left for Lincoln. Tunstall's men retrieved the body, which they carried on horseback to Lincoln.

The Las Vegas Optic reported a third version of the shooting. It said that Middleton, Brewer, Widenmann and Bonney had accompanied John Tunstall from his ranch on the Rio Feliz to Lincoln to turn over a herd of horses that had been attached by Sheriff Brady. As they crested a hill, they saw a large group of horsemen moving quickly toward them. After several shots were fired in their direction, the four men fled for cover on a rocky hillside. Middleton encouraged Tunstall to flee from the approaching horsemen, but Tunstall decided to stay and explain his position.

Dick Brewer said that three shots were heard from where he had taken cover on a hillside behind some rocks. They immediately assumed that Tunstall had been killed. Brewer thought the posse's intention was to kill them all. Later, two more shots were heard.

When the posse had left, the four men returned to find Tunstall dead on the road. He had been shot once in the back of the head and once in the chest. It appeared that his head had been bashed in by a rifle butt. Tunstall's horse had been shot in the head. The two bodies lay side by side. Tunstall's coat had been placed under his head as a pillow. His hat was under the dead horse's head. It was as if the two had stopped to take a nap along the road.

According to Brewer, Tunstall's men found the Englishman's pistol lying next to him. Two shots had been fired from the gun. Brewer thought that the two subsequent shots that he had heard were fired from Tunstall's gun to make the impression that he had fired at the posse.

A following article said that Brewer, Widenmann, Middleton and Bonney took Tunstall's body to Lincoln. They sought out

Justice of the Peace, John B. Wilson. Tunstall's four men signed affidavits as to what they had witnessed. Wilson then organized a coroner's inquest.

The coroner's jury concluded that John Tunstall's death was likely to have been murder. Afterwards, Wilson swore out warrants for the arrest of Jimmy Dolan, Jesse Evans and sixteen others who were implicated in the Tunstall murder. Wilson also swore out warrants for Sheriff Brady and his deputies for looting the Tunstall store.

Wilson turned the warrants over to Constable Atanacio Martinez. The next morning, Martinez deputized William Bonney and Fred Waite to help with the arrest of Sheriff Brady as well as members of the posse who were suspects in the Tunstall murder. When the three men arrived at the House, an armed force was waiting for them. Their weapons were confiscated. Bonney, Waite and Constable Martinez were thrown in the underground pit.

This was all the information that the three papers had about the murder of John Tunstall. I could picture Billy marching down the street with his revolver and Winchester, thinking that the three of them could arrest Sheriff Brady and his small army. Billy and the others had followed the law, but there was no law in Lincoln County.

9

Several days after I had read the account of Billy being deputized and then thrown in jail, three buffalo hunters entered the post office at Sunnyside. The buffalo hunt on the Southern Plains had finally played out. Millions of buffalo had been reduced to a scattered few thousand. Susan called it a senseless slaughter. I thought it had to do with forcing the plains Indians onto reservations.

The three men looked like they had not been anywhere near civilization for quite some time. The tall one, maybe six foot-five in height had come in to post a letter to Louisiana. His name was Pat Garrett. He had an air of self-importance. I would later learn that his family had owned a plantation that was seized by the Union Army during the war. His family had lost all of its property.

Garrett did all the talking. The other two had

the surely look of men who were down on their luck. Garret inquired about work in the area. I told him that Pete Maxwell owned the town and all the land around it. He and John Chisum were the only employers between Puerto de Luna and Roswell. Garrett thanked me and the three men left for Fort Sumner.

I was hoping that someone from Lincoln might pass through Sunnyside with information about the Tunstall murder. In mid-February, with a foot of snow on the ground and a cold wind blowing from the north, no one was on the road unless he had to be.

On Friday, the stage from Las Vegas arrived. I read the Santa Fe paper first. A detachment of troops had been sent from Fort Stanton to Lincoln to aid Constable Martinez in the arrest of Sheriff Brady and his deputies who had looted the Tunstall store. Billy and Fred Waite had been freed from jail after two days.

The next day, Brady and his deputies were released on bond and the troops returned to Fort Stanton. Control of the Tunstall store has been turned over to Alexander McSween. This had become a standoff between Tunstall's small group of men, including Billy, and the much larger force under Sheriff Brady who had the support of District Attorney Rynerson and

121

District Judge Bristol. It began to seem unlikely that there would be any prosecutions for the murder of John Tunstall.

When I read the Las Vegas Daily Optic's account of recent events, a clearer picture emerged. It reported that when Constable Martinez confronted Sheriff Brady about why he had arrested William Bonney and Fred Waite and why he refused to arrest any of the men with outstanding warrants in the Tunstall murder, Brady simply answered, "Because I have the power."

The report stated that Bonney and Waite had their weapons confiscated and had been generally abused by Brady's men while they were incarcerated for two days. I remembered Billy's account of suffering similar abuse by the blacksmith at Fort Grant. That rude behavior had not ended well for the blacksmith. I doubted that Billy would forget this matter.

Late in February 1878, a spotted sheep dog showed up at the post office. I almost stepped on him when I went out to cross the road for supper. He looked cold and hungry.

"C'mon," I motioned for him to follow me around to the back of the house. I led him into the lean-to that we used for laundry and a wash area.

"Stay," I said and went into the house.

"We have a visitor," I told Susan.

"Who is it?" She looked out from the kitchen.

"It's not a who. Have a look."

When Susan entered the small back room, her face lit up as she crouched down to pet the dog, "You poor boy. Where did you come from? You must be hungry."

She went to the kitchen and ladled out a bowl of beef from the stew that was cooking and returned to the lean-to. "You won't understand, but we have to let this cool off a little," she went back to stroking the dog's neck. "It's not quite done, but I doubt that you'll mind."

After the stew had cooled, we watched the hungry dog wolf down every bite and lick the bowl clean. Susan had always had a dog when she was growing up in Chicago. I realized that this might be just the tonic to help her get through the winter.

After he had eaten, I figured that the old dog might like to warm up by the fire. We went inside and he flopped down in front of the fireplace. He didn't take his eyes off either of us as we ate our supper. I could see he was fighting sleep, but he didn't want to let us out of his sight. From that night forward, Lonesome Joe was my wife's constant companion.

The next week's Santa Fe paper reported that Sheriff Brady had arrested fifteen individuals aligned with Tunstall. They were arrested for rioting, but they had to be released, as the Lincoln jail could not accommodate them.

The Las Vegas Gazette reported that John Chisum had been released from jail in Las Vegas and had returned to his South Springs ranch. The story said that he had sent a cattle detective, named Frank McNabb, to help Constable Martinez locate the suspects in the Tunstall Murder.

The Optic contained more detailed information. It reported that Justice of the Peace, John Wilson, had appointed Dick Brewer, Tunstall's ranch foreman, as a special constable. In turn, he deputized William Bonney and gathered a posse of about twenty men to hunt for John Tunstall's killers.

These new lawmen call themselves "The Regulators." They had quickly moved east to the Pecos in search of those with outstanding murder warrants. With the help of detective McNabb, they wanted to strike while the iron was hot.

Another piece in the Optic described a twelve foot high adobe wall that Lawyer McSween was building around his house to counter a possible siege by Sheriff Brady's men. McSween told the reporter that there is no longer any law in the town of Lincoln.

10

As the calendar turned to March, the weather became more agreeable. There was still an occasional cold wind, but most of the snow had melted off. Spring was close at hand. Susan had arranged with Pete Maxwell to set up a small classroom at Fort Sumner. In turn, Maxwell provided her with a buggy and a docile mule to pull it.

From dawn until dark, Lonesome Joe was at Susan's side. He would hop onto the floor of the buggy and off they would go to Sumner. Joe would take a forward position and keep his eyes fixed on the road as the navigator. The old spotted dog had found the Promised Land. He ate whatever we ate and spent his nights stretched out in front of the fire.

When the southbound stage arrived on

Friday, I scanned the newspapers to learn what had happened in Lincoln. The first article in the Santa Fe paper was disturbing.

The Regulators had gone to the Pecos in search of men who had warrants for the murder of John Tunstall. They had jumped a group of five Dolan men on the Rio Penasco, south of Roswell. A running battle ensued with the Dolan men splitting into two groups. The Regulators chose to pursue Buck Morton, who was suspected of firing the shot that killed Tunstall, and Frank Baker, who was a member of the Jesse Evans Gang and a member of the posse that day.

When their horses finally gave out, Morton and Baker took cover in a stand of trees. When their ammunition began to run low, they surrendered to Constable Dick Brewer who assured them that they would be taken back to Lincoln without harm.

The Brewer posse took the two prisoners up the Pecos to the Gilbert ranch. William McCloskey who was a personal friend of both Morton and Baker joined them. He promised the two fugitives that he would see that they reached Lincoln safely.

The posse then rode north to John Chisum's South Springs Ranch where they stayed the night. The Regulators were told that they might be intercepted by a group of Dolan's men before they could reach Lincoln.

The next morning, the Regulators and their two prisoners headed west along the Hondo toward Lincoln. Fearing intervention by Dolan's men, the Regulators decided to take a less used trail through Agua Negra Canyon. According to the New Mexican, Morton, Baker and McCloskey were murdered there.

This was damning news as far as Billy was concerned. If the Brewer posse had executed the three men before they reached Lincoln, no explanation would be acceptable.

There was a second article in the New Mexican that made the first story more troubling. It seemed that while the Brewer posse was arresting Morton and Baker, Governor Axtell had come to Lincoln and removed Justice of the Peace John Wilson from his position. This rendered all processes that he had issued to be void. This meant that Brewer and his posse were acting without legal authority in the arrest of Morton and Baker.

Harold's reporting in the Las Vegas Daily Optic had additional details that had been omitted by the Santa Fe paper. The Optic reported that William McCloskey had gotten into an argument with Frank McNabb, who was the stock detective sent by John Chisum to help track down John Tunstall's killers.

At some point in the argument, guns were drawn and McCloskey was shot and killed. At this point, Morton and Baker attempted to escape. They had no chance to outrun the posse. They were chased by the Regulators and shot out of their saddles.

The next week's New Mexican was full of angry pronouncements against this "band of killers" led by Dick Brewer. The New Mexican demanded that the full force of the territory would be required to bring this lawless element to justice. Suddenly forgotten was the murder of John Tunstall.

The Optic reported that Jesse Evans had been arrested again. He had shot a man during the attempted robbery of a sheep camp. Evans and his confederate, Tom Hill, had ridden into John Wagner's camp on the Tularosa River. They had engaged in a shoot out with a Cherokee Indian who had been left to guard the camp.

Tom Hill was killed while Evans took a bullet to the left elbow. Constable Dave Wood later discovered Evans on the trail. Evans was arrested and taken to the Fort Stanton stockade where he received medical attention.

The Las Vegas Gazette reported that Dick Brewer's men were hiding in San Patricio, just east of Lincoln. This was an Hispano settlement where Constable Chavez y Chavez was the only officer of the law left in Lincoln County who was not controlled by Thomas Catron or Jimmy Dolan.

During the last part of the March, there were no reports of any violence in Lincoln. The Regulators were in San Patricio among their Mexican supporters. Lawyer McSween and his wife were enjoying the safety of the fortress known as the South Springs Ranch. There was no mention of Billy's whereabouts. I assumed he was with his friends at San Patricio.

11

Near the end of March, Harold Early rode into Sunnyside. I walked out onto the road to meet him as he got down off his tall mule.

"My god, it's a mess down there," He said with a tired voice. "And the worst may be yet to come."

"Surely Billy and the rest of them will have the good sense to clear out of there."

"No," Harold took off his broad brimmed hat and wiped his forehead. "Chisum has hired that little group of fighters to protect McSween when he returns to Lincoln. I'm sure Uncle John will remain in the safety of his South Springs Ranch. It's nothing short of suicide for them to return to Lincoln, but these Tunstall boys have their backs up and they don't seem to be troubled by the odds. I had to get out of there for a couple of days."

"I read about Morton and Baker. So Billy is right in the middle of it?"

"Hell yes. He spent two days in jail. He had been arrested when he went to the House to arrest Dolan and his men with Constable Martinez and Fred Waite. While they were down in the pit, I was told they were pissed on from above by Brady's men.

"When Billy was released, Brady wouldn't give him his Winchester and revolver back. These were weapons that John Tunstall had given him. So Billy borrows a gun belt and a rifle from Dick Brewer and challenges three of Brady's deputies to settle up with him in the street. Billy told them it would be a fair fight. By this time there was a crowd on both sides of the street.

Billy waited for several minutes. There were no takers. There was lot of shuffling and nervous faces on the other side of the street. Billy was angry about the abuse he had endured in lockup for two days. Who could blame him? This kid has nerve, but I wonder about his good sense."

"I saw that same thing at Puerto de Luna. He has no fear."

"Not this boy," Harold shook his head. "I don't know if it's anger about the Englishman or his treatment by Brady's men, but he's in a bloody mood and nobody will stand up to him."

"Playing to the crowd may get him killed one day," I had been thinking about that since Puerto de Luna.

"He'll likely hang unless somebody shoots him in the back," was Harold's conclusion.

"It's a shame he found himself in the middle of all this," I said. "He and Fred Waite had been looking to acquire a piece of land down on the Penasco."

"Well," Harold said as he led Moses to the stable, "That's all over now. He ought to run and run fast. Instead, the damn fools are going to accompany McSween back to Lincoln. Your traveling reporter will no doubt be there to witness the carnage."

Harold pulled the saddle and bridal off of Moses and reached into his war sack. "Have a nip," he offered me the flask.

"Here's to the Regulators," I said as I took a swallow and handed the flask to Harold.

He thought for a moment, "Here's to the day when we see an honest politician in Santa Fe." He took a good long pull. "This is all their doing. The rest of these poor devils are like

133

discards in a poker game."

"Let's go see what Susan has in mind for supper. She'll be glad to see you."

When we got to the house, Lonesome Joe was there to greet us.

"A new boarder," Harold asked as he patted the dog on the head.

"He showed up half starved this winter."

"He's probably finer company than some dusty traveler from Kentucky." You could hear the weariness in Harold's voice.

"He's been just the remedy for Susan this winter. He eats less than you, but he's not nearly as entertaining."

"That might be the closest thing to a compliment that I'll ever get from you, ya little Mick."

"Susan," I called as we entered to house. "A traveling dignitary has arrived."

Susan came out of the kitchen. Her face lit up when she saw Harold. "Well, Mr. Early," she smiled. "It's about time you stopped by."

"I suppose this has become my safe haven," Harold grinned.

"You two make yourselves comfortable," she motioned to the chairs by the fireplace. "I'm afraid it's just stew."

"I'd be happy if it was salt pork belly,"

Harold said as he took a seat.

"In your mind, what will be the outcome down there," I asked as I reached for the good whiskey and two glasses. I sat down opposite the big fellow and poured us each a glass.

"You'd think that McSween and Tunstall's men would have the good sense to clear out, but it's not going that direction," Harold explained. "Many of those boys own land south of Lincoln. McSween has that fancy adobe place in town. They call it 'The Castle', for Christ's sake. The damn fool has been writing letters to President Hays, protesting the corruption and asking for federal protection. There's only so much the troops from Fort Stanton can do.

"You have the Jesse Evans bunch, although he's in the stockade at Fort Stanton right now. They're hired killers. Nothing more. Then you have the so-called Seven Rivers Warriors, who are mostly small cattlemen who hate John Chisum. They're a cut above the Evans bunch, but just as deadly. Bill Rynerson, the district prosecutor, is in Catron's hip pocket. The word is that Rynerson has given Jimmy Dolan the go ahead to get rid of McSween and the Regulators by any means necessary.

"If McSween tries to take back his home in Lincoln, at the encouragement of Chisum, the outcome is predictable. They'll be killed and Catron will have his fiefdom back in place. It's that simple.

"I'll head back down that way tomorrow. I'll be on hand for the bloodiest thing ever seen in these parts. I don't see any chance of a cheerful outcome."

We ate supper without any more talk of the pending battle in Lincoln. We talked about our families in Chicago and Kentucky. Together, we wondered about the odd circumstances that had brought us together in this strange territory out west.

"You know, my daddy's farm in Hardin County is less than a mile from where Abe Lincoln grew up," Harold said as he mopped up the last bit of gravy with a biscuit.

"I knew it," I was feeling content from the whiskey and the good food. "There was greatness in that soil. Abe achieved a level of notoriety, but his accomplishments pale in comparison with yours."

Harold laughed. "The closest I'll come to any position of importance is if I end up as editor of the Optic when Old Man Hersh steps down."

"So that's your intention," Susan asked.

"It would be a step up. I could ride Moses through town and strike fear into the hearts of all the miscreants. Maybe take Tom Catron to task for all his evil deeds."

"We couldn't blame you for wanting to sleep in a clean bed every night," Susan agreed.

"Is Hersh intending to step down," I asked.

"I don't know, Harold played down the subject. "He'll still be drooling pipe spit down his chin whiskers as long as he's vertical, but he's seventy-seven. His drooling days may be numbered."

"That's a flattering picture of your employer," I said.

"In all fairness," Harold became serious. "He's about the only halfway honest editor in these parts. He's too old to be afraid of Catron. He prides himself in presenting a different slant on things. In truth, I have great respect for the old man. He wouldn't have us spew the lies that are required at the New Mexican. For that, I'm grateful."

Harold was half asleep in his chair at this point so we decided to turn in for the night. I looked forward to watching Susan getting ready for bed while Harold had to be content with a night on the plank floor, along side Lonesome Joe. I shouldn't have taken satisfaction in that, but I did.

12

By the end of the first week in April, Harold's expectations had begun to materialize. All three papers printed nearly the same story. Sheriff William Brady and Deputy George Hindman had been shot down in the street by six of John Tunstall's men. William Bonney was one of the shooters.

So there it was. Billy had been involved in the killing of an elected officer of the law. The fact that Brady and Hindman were wanted for the murder of John Tunstall made little difference. The Regulators had crossed the line. They would have to leave the territory or face deadly consequences.

The Optic made the point that with Brady dead, none of his deputies had any authority under the law. Now, there was literally no law in Lincoln. It was also clear that Tunstall's men would not rest until all of those involved with his murder had been dealt with.

The Optic stated that Billy Bonney and Fred Waite had been wounded in the exchange of gunfire with Brady's men. Billy had run into the street to recover the revolver and Winchester that Brady had taken from him. He had taken a bullet to the thigh. He managed to get to his horse and follow the other Regulators to San Patricio. Fred Waite had a more serious injury to his leg. He crawled into the Tunstall Store where his wound was treated by a Dr. Ealy. He was then hidden under a trap door in the floor.

Late that night, despite his injured leg, Billy rode alone back to Lincoln. Bonney got Waite onto his horse and they rode to San Patricio. Billy could easily have sent someone else to collect Waite, but he chose to do it himself. This reinforced a conclusion that I had come to about the boy. He would always do what he thought was honorable, even if it made no sense.

Susan's classroom had finally been finished. Some of the Mexican men at Sumner were able to cut down three long tables and about twenty chairs to the children's size. Wood was delivered to use in the fireplace. More children would show up for class each day until more chairs were needed. Pete Maxwell ordered a blackboard from St. Louis. By the end of April, Susan's makeshift school was in full operation.

Every morning at seven, I would harness the mule. Susan would set off in the buggy down the road to Fort Sumner. Lonesome Joe sat directly in front of her on the floor to help with directions. The old sheep dog would lie under her desk all day until it was time to return home.

Susan's good-natured ways had returned with her new teaching duties. She was more fun to be around, particularly at night. For that, I was eternally grateful. I suppose she needed some sense of accomplishment other than doing laundry and cooking supper.

The spring weather was near perfect. I spent the days making repairs on the two adobe buildings and the stable. When Susan returned home in the late afternoon, I would show her my handiwork and she would tell me about the children at school. She had learned a little Spanish since we had come to New Mexico and the children knew a little English. It was an imperfect arrangement, but the children were excited to be in school.

During the month of April, the reports from Lincoln diminished. There were no more battles involving the Regulators until a story appeared from Blazer's Mill. The Regulators had gotten into a gunfight with Andrew Roberts, who had been a member of the posse that had killed John Tunstall. Roberts had recently been involved in a long distance shoot out with Billy Bonney and Charlie Bowdre outside of San Patricio.

During the exchange of gunfire at Blazer's Mill, Charlie Bowdre had shot Roberts in the gut. As Roberts returned fire with his Winchester, a bullet hit Bowdre in the belt buckle. Bowdre escaped serious injury, but his gun belt had been shot off of him. Another shot from Roberts took off George Coe's index finger on his right hand.

Roberts managed to crawl through a door and set up a mattress as a fort in the doorway. When he had run out of ammunition, Roberts discovered Dr. Blazer's Sharps buffalo rifle. Roberts was a crack shot and the Regulators were reluctant to show themselves.

As the standoff dragged on, Dick Brewer circled around the log yard to get a clear view of the doorway where Roberts was barricaded. He fired into the doorway, which allowed Roberts to see the rifle smoke come up from behind the logs. When Roberts saw Brewer's hat appear above the logs, he shot Brewer through the head.

With Roberts dying and their leader killed, the Regulators left Blazers Mill and rode north. The next day, Roberts and Brewer were buried side by side on a hill above Blazer's Mill.

Then came reports of indictments from a grand jury in Mesilla. Billy Bonney, Henry Brown and John Middleton were indicted for the murder of Sheriff Brady. Fred Waite was indicted for the murder of Deputy Hindman. Frank McNabb and Jim French, the other two Regulators present at the Brady shooting, were not indicted.

Charlie Bowdre was indicted for the murder of Buckshot Roberts. Eight other Regulators were indicted as accessories. Jesse Evans and five others were indicted for the murder of John Tunstall. Jimmy Dolan and Deputy Billy Matthews were indicted as accessories. Dolan and his new partner, Johnny Riley, were indicted for cattle theft.

The grand jury decided not to indict Alexander McSween on embezzlement charges. With all of his business partners under indictment, Lawrence Murphy had gone to Fort Stanton to seek protection.

Toward the end of April, there were reports of a fight between the Regulators and the Seven Rivers Warriors near the Fritz Ranch. Chisum's cattle detective, Frank McNabb, had assumed leadership of the Regulators after the death of Dick Brewer. McNab, Ab Saunders and Frank Coe were apparently ambushed by the Seven Rivers mob. McNab was killed. Coe and Saunders were wounded.

At dawn, the next morning, the Regulators surprised the Seven Rivers Warriors. Five of the Warriors were killed. The battle ended when troops from Fort Stanton arrived and positioned themselves between the two factions. The reports indicated that the Regulators were holding their own in the Lincoln County War.

Another piece in the New Mexican declared that Lawrence Murphy and Jimmy Dolan had abandoned all of their operations in Lincoln. Their entire holdings had been turned over to Thomas Catron and the First National Bank of Santa Fe. Had Tunstall and McSween waited a few more months before setting up their operation in Lincoln, there may have been no war. They might have won by default.

13

Through the month of May, there was little to report from Lincoln County. A man by the name of John Copeland had assumed the job of sheriff. By all accounts, he was an impartial official. Lawrence Murphy had left the area for good. Jimmie Dolan was facing a number of indictments, although he could expect a sympathetic treatment from District Prosecutor William Rynerson and District Judge Warren Bristol.

By the end of May, Governor Axtell had dismissed Sheriff Copeland had replaced him with a former Brady deputy named George Peppin. The new sheriff was a Dolan supporter. Impartial law enforcement in Lincoln had lasted one month.

Pat Garrett, the former buffalo hunter, had

become a regular at Sunnyside. He would come into the post office and ask to read the papers. He wasn't much for conversation. He would sit in a high backed chair and stretch out his long legs. His face was always behind the paper. I would go about my business until he finished reading. He would thank me and leave.

Garrett had opened a small cafe and saloon, possibly with money loaned to him by Pete Maxwell. When the business failed, he opened up a butcher shop with Barney Mason. They seemed to be doing well until it was discovered that they were carving up stolen beef. Garrett then went to work as a bartender for Beaver Smith.

It seemed to me that Garrett was determined to rise above the status of buffalo hunter and card player, but there were few opportunities at this isolated settlement. After he had fallen out of the good graces of Pete Maxwell, he had been reduced to bartender and gambler.

Garrett spent most of his time in one of the two small saloons at Fort Sumner. Beaver Smith's gambling hall was at the southwest corner of the old fort. Bob Hargrove held down the northeast corner of the fort with his whiskey palace. They were the only games in town. Neither offered much more than whiskey and dust.

Pat Garrett wasn't a particularly good card player. He had squandered two years of earnings from his buffalo killing days and had arrived at Fort Sumner without a dollar to his name. He had the bearing of an aristocrat, but, as Harold would say, he didn't have a proverbial pot to piss in. The word was that he owed money around town. I was waiting for the day when he tried to put the arm on me.

I early June, we got another letter from Billy.

Dear Robert and Susan,

We've been holed up at the Chisum Ranch or in San Patricio which is the only placita still friendly to us. We've been in a fight the last four months with those who killed John.

Looking forward to the day when we can head north and be done with this business. We are mostly here to protect McSween and his wife as without us they would surely be killed.

Yours, Billy

Susan was pleased to hear from Billy. It reinforced her hope that he could somehow put the war in Lincoln County behind him. I thought that the only way he could accomplish a new start was to get a long way away from New Mexico.

A few days after we had received the letter, a young man appeared in the doorway of the post office. When he tipped back his sombrero, I was startled to see Billy.

"You look like a man who just bumped into a ghost," Billy smiled.

"I'm surprised to see you, Billy," I admitted as I walked around the counter to shake hands. "You look pretty damn healthy considering all the ground you've covered lately."

"What do the papers say about us?"

"There are always different versions. You'll never get a fair shake in the Santa Fe paper. The Gazette is worthless, but Optic gives a pretty square account of things. I'm sure you've met their reporter. Harold Early."

"I bump into him everywhere. The first time was at Seven Rivers when I was staying at the Jones place. He's a good ol' Irishman who gets on with all my friends. More than once, he's gotten fall down drunk with us. We try to stay on his friendly side to encourage a favorable reporting."

"He's an honest fella," I welcomed the chance to put in a good word for Harold. "He knows about every bit of corruption from Santa Fe to Lincoln. I know the whole story of Catron and Murphy because of him."

"You know, Robert, there was never any chance that those who killed John were going be prosecuted. Rynerson and Judge Bristol are in the Dolan camp. For a short time, I was a deputy constable under Dick Brewer. Can you picture that? The whole thing is so rotten that we had to take matters into our own hands. We've finished five of those who killed John and I expect we'll get a few more."

"Wouldn't it be a good plan to call the thing finished and get out of the territory?"

"If we cleared out now, McSween is a dead man. Maybe his wife, too. Evans and that bunch have no honor when it comes to a thing like that. And they're being encouraged by Rynerson to get rid of the whole lot of us."

"I'm worried that with Catron calling the shots, the whole territory will be lined up against you."

"That may be true, but we can't run. Not just yet."

"Where's Gracie?" As soon as I had asked

the question, I wished I hadn't.

Billy shook his head. "That's a sad tale, Robert. And I hate to tell it. She broke a leg down on the Ruidoso. She stepped in a badger hole and snapped her right foreleg in two. We were at a full gallop. She threw me fifteen feet.

"She never struggled to get up the way a horse usually will. She stayed there on the ground, breathing hard as I went up to her. She just lay there and looked up at me with those intelligent eyes. I bent down and stroked her neck to tell her it was okay. She just looked up at me. She trusted me to do what was right. That's what really got me. That trust she had in her eyes."

"Jesus, Billy, I'm sorry I asked."

"There'll never be another mare like Gracie. Shooting her was the most miserable thing I ever had to do. She was as much a friend as any human could be. Better than most, I'd say."

"She was something," Was all I could think of to say.

"That sorrel's race bred, but he's no Gracie," Billy looked out the door at the gelding tied to the post. "He belonged to Brady. After what he put me and Fred through in the pit for two days, I figured he owed me his horse."

Billy turned back to face me. "I would have

dug her a grave if I had anything to work with. I spent the morning piling rocks over her to keep the crows and coyotes off. I'll never forget that intelligent mare."

"You want to stay for supper? Susan will be home in an hour or so."

"No. As much as I'd like to see her, it's best if I don't get spotted alone by those I'm at odds with. Tell her not to think bad of me for all the killing that's went on. The Dolan crowd gave us no selection. That's the short of it. Maybe when this is all over, we can have that cup of tea," Billy reached out his hand.

"We'd like that, Billy," I said. "Where you off to?"

"If it was anyone else, I wouldn't be inclined to say," Billy looked me in the eye. "I'm heading up to Puerto de Luna. To see Hortencia. I couldn't sit around South Springs another day. I expect Will Chisum and I have caught every fish there was in that stretch of the Pecos. Sally is fond of me, but she's so hot and cold, I never know which way to jump."

"Hortencia will be happy to see you. Esmeralda may want to adopt you. You could run around barefoot with Tito."

Billy dropped his head and laughed. "I could do worse. Those are nice folks up there."

"You watch things close, Billy"

Billy turned and walked out to his horse. He quickly hopped into the saddle. With a wave of his sombrero, he headed north along the river.

I felt gloomy to see Billy for such a short time. He always put me in good spirits. He looked healthy. He had gained some weight. He seemed a little more serious. More grown up, I suppose. My young friend did not lack courage. He was certainly at risk as he traveled alone to Puerto de Luna. Maybe the only thing that Billy feared was to be idle.

14

During the last part of June and early July, 1878, there were several accounts of skirmishes between the Regulators and those working for the new sheriff, George Peppin. Most of the battles occurred around San Patricio where the Regulators had the support of the local Hispanos. Frank McNabb, the cattle detective who had replaced Dick Brewer as leader of the Regulators, had been killed. The Santa Fe paper reported that William Bonney was now in charge.

Sheriff Pepin had inherited the support of Jesse Evans and the Seven Rivers Warriors. At the behest of District Prosecutor William Rynerson, John Kinney and his band of outlaws had come from Mesilla to aid Peppin.

The Regulators had recruited new forces from the Mexican community who would fight for any side opposed to the Jimmy Dolan faction. For a time, Peppin was able to gain the support of troops from Fort Stanton, but the new Posse Comitatis Act, which forbade the use of the U.S military against civilians, put an end to Colonel Dudley's assistance.

The Optic reported on the Jesse Evans trial in Mesilla. Evans was being tried for the murder of John Tunstall. The paper said that Judge Warren Bristol stopped just short of calling Rob Widenmann a liar. Widenmann was the key eyewitness who had been with Tunstall the day he was killed.

Prosecutor William Rynerson, a friend of Evans and a supporter of Jimmy Dolan, was reported to be offering less than an enthusiastic prosecution of Evans. The trial was postponed and Evans walked away on five thousand dollars bail. That was quite a piece of change for a hired killer.

The Optic reported that former Lincoln Sheriff John Copeland had gone to Fort Stanton to seek protection from the current sheriff in Lincoln. It seemed as though the fun never ended in Lincoln. The same article reported that Alexander McSween and his wife had left San

Patricio for the protection of John Chisum's ranch.

It turned out that McSween's timing was excellent. Several days after his departure, John Kinney and his gang turned San Patricio upside down. Livestock was killed, the Dowling Store was looted and houses were burned down. According to the Optic reporter, this was a warning to the town to no longer harbor the Regulators. It was reported that Sheriff Peppin had sanctioned the attack on San Patricio.

The following week, there were reports of a siege at Chisum's South Springs Ranch. Peppin's deputy, Buck Powell, had been sent to Roswell to bring in the Regulators. Shots had been exchanged during the day and into the night with no casualties on either side.

With the Regulators pinned down near Roswell, John Kinney cashed in on the opportunity to loot the ranches of George and Frank Coe as well as the ranch of Ab Saunders. The Regulators now found themselves in a position where they could not protect their own property.

The last two weeks of July, all three papers were filled with reports about a five-day battle in Lincoln. When it had ended, McSween was dead and his large compound had been burned to the ground.   A handful of Regulators, including William Bonney, had escaped the fire and fled across the Rio Bonito and into the night.

When Alexander McSween decided to return to his home in Lincoln, John Chisum had enlisted the Regulators to protect him.   The group had also picked up the support of Martin Chavez and his group of fighters who where angry about the sacking of San Patricio.

The small army of nearly sixty men arrived in Lincoln just after dark on the night of July 14, 1878.   They took up positions in the Tunstall Store, the Montano Store and the Ellis house at the east end of town. The core of the Regulators took up positions in the McSween home.   The idea was to drive Sheriff Peppin and his men from town if they tied to force McSween from his home.

When Sheriff Peppin discovered the size of the force that McSween has brought to Lincoln, he sent messengers out to bring his three gangs back to town.   When they had the McSween positions surrounded, the shooting began.   Shots were exchanged throughout the day.   Nightfall brought a temporary end to the fighting.

On the second day, the fighting continued. A messenger from Colonel Dudley at Fort Stanton had reported back to Dudley that he had been fired on by the Regulators. The messenger had also brought a request from Jimmy Dolan for the use of a mountain howitzer to force the McSween men from their positions. Dudley, however, was reluctant to aid Sheriff Peppin because of the recently enacted Posse Comitatus Act.

On the third day, each side had one man shot. This had become a standoff with no end in sight. Dudley sent five soldiers to Lincoln to appraise the situation. They found the entire town forted up. The troops reportedly came under fire by unknown shooters. When they arrived back at Fort Stanton, Dudley sent a message to Peppin that he would bring his forces from Fort Stanton to restore order.

On the fifth day of the standoff, Colonel Dudley arrived in Lincoln with thirty-five men and three days worth of provisions. He brought along the mountain howitzer and a Gatling gun with two thousand rounds of ammunition. As the sound of drums was heard west of town, the gunfire subsided.

When Sheriff Peppin met with the colonel at the west edge of town, Dudley warned him that if either side fired at his men, they would be annihilated. As the army moved through town,

Peppin's men were able to take up better positions in houses that surrounded the McSween home.

After Dudley had set up camp, he had the howitzer pointed at the front of the Montano Store. Fearing that they were about to be blasted out of the store, the McSween men quickly left the building and fled east to the Ellis house.

When Dudley got word that two groups of Regulators were in the Ellis house, he gave word to a Lieutenant Goodwin to move the howitzer and aim it at the front of the Ellis house. When the men inside the house saw the business end of the howitzer pointed directly at them, they scrambled out the back of the house to the corral. They saddled their horses and fled across the Rio Bonito and into the hills to the north.

When Sheriff Peppin saw the band of about forty men abandon the Ellis house, he went in and confiscated the rifles and ammunition that had been left behind. In the corral were the thirteen horses belonging to the men left in the McSween home. With the McSween house surrounded by the army and most of their confederates driven from town, the remaining Regulators were in a hopeless position.

In the early afternoon on the fifth day, Peppin

decided to set fire to the McSween home. When Susan McSween saw that her home was about to be torched, she bravely walked up the street to Dudley's camp. She confronted Colonel Dudley as to why her house was surrounded by the U.S. Army.

Dudley explained that he was there only to protect women and children. When Mrs. McSween explained that there were women and children inside her house, Dudley told her that they would not be safe until she forced the Regulators out of the house.

Peppin and his men made several attempts to start a fire. They finally got a good burn going on the west end. As the house was primarily adobe, the progress of the fire was slow. Inside, the men pulled up floorboards to rob the fire of fuel, but the smoke was becoming a problem.

At the urging of William Bonney, Susan McSween again met with Dudley to ask for protection of the two women and five children that remained in the McSween home. Colonel Dudley agreed to safely escort them to a position of safety. As evening fell on the Rio Bonito Valley, two thirds of Alexander McSween's home had been burned. Only the kitchen area at the northeast corner remained and it was on fire.

According to reports from those left in the burning house, at around nine o'clock that night, William Bonney conceived a plan of escape. He and four others would leave the house and fire at the enemy as they ran toward the Tunstall store. This would create a diversion and draw the fire of Peppin's men. Meanwhile, McSween and the others were to escape out the back and across the river.

As soon as Billy's group ran for the Tunstall Store, they were spotted in the light of the burning house. Before they could get to the store, they were caught in a hail of bullets. Harvey Morris was shot in the head and killed. He was a consumptive who had decided to stay and fight. Bonney returned fire and hit John Kinney in the side of the face. When they got to the Tunstall store, they were met by three soldiers and a number of Dolan men.

The four men then decided to make for the Rio Bonito. Inside the store, the three remaining Regulators saw their friends heading for the river. They fled through the back door and were able to scale an adobe wall and join the other four. The seven men crossed the river and scattered into the hills.

Inside the burning house, Lawyer McSween and the others had waited too long to make their exit. The group fell under heavy gunfire. McSween raised his hands and said he wanted to surrender.

Deputy Robert Beckwith approached the group. He told McSween that he would be allowed to surrender. As he approached the lawyer, McSween yelled that he would never surrender. At the same moment, Beckwith was hit twice by bullets and killed. As soon as Beckwith fell, McSween was shot five times. He fell on top of Beckwith.

Two more of McSween's men were killed behind the house, but six others made it to the safety of the river. Yginio Salazar was thought to be dead. He lay motionless for several hours. When the street finally cleared, he managed to crawl half a mile to his sister-in-law's home. Gunfire had ended. The Lincoln County War was over.

The next day, the bodies of Alexander McSween and Harvey Morris were buried behind the Tunstall Store along side the graves of John Tunstall and Frank McNab. They were buried without coffins or a change of clothes.

15

Our friend Harold arrived in Sunnyside in early August. He was on his way to Las Vegas to assume the editor's position at the Daily Optic. His spirits were high. He would no longer have to travel the southern part of the territory in search of news. Harold had been a witness to the five-day battle in Lincoln. He thought the Regulators were very fortunate to have survived the siege.

Harold told us of a new gang that had come in from Texas to take advantage of the disarray in Lincoln County. They called themselves Selman's Scouts. The gang had looted stores and homes from Lincoln to La Junta. They had also sacked the ranches of Frank Coe and Ab Saunders.

Selman's Scouts rode onto the Chavez Ranch. They shot three young Mexican boys out of their saddles and stole their horses. The Selman gang then stole horses from the Sanchez ranch and killed another young boy. For good measure, the gang raped two women at Bartlett's Mill, near Lincoln. Satisfied with their plunder, Selman's Scouts crossed back into Texas.

Harold said that this was the worst bunch he had encountered during his six years in the territory. Jessie Evans and John Kinney were thieves and killers, but they stopped short of killing children and raping women. The Seven Rivers Warriors were not opposed to killing. They were angry about having their grazing land swallowed up by John Chisum.

Harold said that the Regulators had lost the five-month war. They had lost their ranches as well. They had fought a good fight, but they had nothing to show for it. To make matters worse, they knew that no one would ever be convicted of the murder of John Tunstall.

With their ranches looted and their livestock stolen, the Regulators, in turn, stole horses and cattle from the big outfits that were opposed to them. In some cases, they were stealing livestock that had been stolen from John Tunstall.

Harold filled in some details about the Regulators that had not made the papers. He

162

said Tom O'Folliard had stopped to try and help Harvey Morris while under heave fire when Morris had been shot in the head. Harold thought that counted for something. He said that Jim French and Charlie Bowdre had gone back to Lincoln after the siege to guard Susan McSween. They feared that she might be killed. Harold said that was honorable to the point of foolishness.

Harold thought that by the time the battle of Lincoln was over, Billy had emerged as the leader of the Regulators. As the McSween home burned down around them, it was Billy who encouraged the others not to give up and it was Billy who planned the escape in which all but three of his men survived. Harold blamed McSween for drawing all of them into a hopeless situation.

When I asked Harold about the future plans of the Regulators, he said that they had gone to the Chisum Ranch. He said Old John was planning to move his cattle up the Pecos into Texas Panhandle. After encouraging John Tunstall to open a mercantile and a bank in Lincoln and compete with the House for cattle contracts, Chisum had decided to move his operation to a more secure location.

Harold said that the Regulators were going to

fall in with Chisum and bring their own sizable herd of horses to sell along the way at Puerto de Luna and Anton Chico. Harold had gotten to know most of the Regulators over the past five months. On more than one occasion, he admitted that he had gotten knee crawling drunk with them. Harold said that he would loan any one of them his last ten dollars. He knew he would get it back.

Susan and I would surely miss seeing Harold ride into Sunnyside on his tall mule. We would miss his unvarnished account of the news and his humor at the supper table.

Harold joked that he was going to be a big shot editor and a man of prestige. He thought he might just go ahead and get married. He was seeing a pretty gal named Luisa. He admitted that he was very fond of her. He thought she would be delighted with his newfound status. Susan and I promised that we would be up to see him. With a tip of the hat, the big Irishman was on his way.

Four days later, as Harold had predicted, word reached us that the Regulators had arrived at Fort Sumner. After supper on Saturday, Susan and I decided to take the buggy into town. There was always a dance on Saturday night at the quartermaster's depot. We figured that this might be a real celebration. For the first time, we would have the chance to take the measure of all the men we had read about in the newspapers.

Susan seemed to be a little nervous as we set off for Fort Sumner. She didn't say two words as the buggy rolled along the sandy road. I guessed that she was pondering all the situations in which Billy had taken part since she had last seen him. Depending on which paper you read, he was a brave boy or a cold killer. As we pulled up at the edge of the parade grounds, we could hear the chorus of a Mexican favorite:

Ay, ay, ay, ay, canta y no llores,
Porque cantando se alegran,
Cielito Lindo, los corezones.

As we entered the long dance hall, there were about forty people there. A line of chairs ran lengthwise on either side of the room. Maybe a dozen pretty Mexican girls sat next to their mothers. Most wore white blouses and colorful skirts. Some held small fans. A considerable amount of time had been taken to make their shining black hair look beautiful. As a finishing touch, most of the girls wore a flower in their hair.

Pete Maxwell's cowhands were standing in two groups, probably discussing how fine the young women looked for this occasion. Susan and I took a seat to the left of the entrance. Pete Maxwell came over and thanked us for coming and expressed his gratitude for Susan taking her time to educate the children in town. She told him that it was her privilege.

The band, consisting of three guitar players and a trumpet player, began to play another Spanish tune. The girls and their mothers looked expectant, but the Mexican men seemed to be in no hurry to get things started. In the far corner, Pat Garrett and Barney Mason appeared to be in a serious discussion.

Several more songs were played until there was a commotion at the doorway as a group of men entered the dance hall. In the lead was Billy with a white shirt and fancy red vest. He wore his trademark black sombrero. As the group came into the room, I noticed the anticipation on the faces of the Mexican girls.

Billy saw us to his left and quickly walked toward us. I stood up.

"I'd like you to meet my pals," Billy looked happy and confident. "Robert and Susan, this is Charley Bowdre. This is my good friend Tom O'Folliard. This is Fred Waite from Oklahoma.

The big fella is Jim French. The two fiddle players are George and Frank Coe. The serious one is Doc Spurlock. Over here is Ab Saunders. I've been riding with these boys for the past six months."

I shook hands all around as the Regulators tipped their hats to Susan. Charlie Bowdre made a bow and kissed the back of her hand. To a man, they had an honest look about them. As a group, they looked like men you would not want to antagonize.

"The O'Dells took me in last fall when I was no more than a leaf blowing up the Pecos," Billy explained to his friends. "Along with Heiskell and Maam Jones, they're as close to family as I've got in these parts."

As the men walked toward the far end of the room, Billy smiled and told Susan, "I haven't forgotten that invitation for tea," He left to join his friends. The Coes had taken a seat with the other four musicians.

When the band began to play a polka, Billy walked over to a pretty Mexican girl seated next to her mother. Billy took off his sombrero and leaned forward. He said something to the mother and she nodded. With that, Billy took the smiling girl by the hand and placed his sombrero on her seat. They walked onto the floor and began to dance. He whisked her around the room with an ease and quickness with here long skirt spinning out around her.

Some of the other Regulators asked women to dance as the floor began to fill with fast moving couples. Several of Pete Maxwell's men took their cue. When Garrett asked a girl to dance, all of the young women had partners.

The song ended and the band began to play a waltz. Billy led the young woman to her seat and leaned forward to say something to her mother. This time, the laughing mother joined Billy on the dance floor. Susan and I decided it was time to get busy. We were caught up in the festive mood as we moved around the floor.

This went on for two hours. If the dance were a polka, Billy would ask another senorita to dance. If it were a waltz, he would ask one of the mothers to join him. When the band finally took a break, Billy came over and asked how we liked the party. Susan told him he was pretty clever to court the mothers along with the daughters. Billy laughed. He said that it was all for fun.

During the break, most of the men went outside to have a pull of whiskey and a smoke. When the band set up again, George and Frank Coe played Turkey in the Straw. Billy asked

Pete Maxwell's younger sister to dance. Paulita might have been the youngest girl at the dance. She looked surprised by the invitation.

Half way through the song, Billy went into an impromptu Irish jig that brought everyone to their feet. As his legs moved faster than legs ought to move, the crowd began to clap. To our left, Tom O'Folliard decided that Billy was not the only Irishman who knew the step.

When Susan poked me in the ribs, I was compelled to show them that a man from Chicago knew a step or two. With the three of us pounding the floor in a somewhat disturbing exhibition, the crowd began to laugh. When the song ended, Billy pointed to me with his best grin. Susan slapped me on the back.

At this point, everyone in the dance hall was laughing and talking loudly. The Mexican men were smiling and shaking their heads as they watched Billy take Paulita back to her chair. Pat Garrett watched Billy from the far side of the room. He, alone, did not seem to be caught in the spirit of the moment.

Part way through the second set, it looked like there might be trouble. Tom O'Folliard had danced with a particularly pretty Mexican girl five or six times. The tall red head seemed to be quite taken with the girl. This seemed to offend some of Maxwell's men. Billy noticed this and pulled Tom off to the side. They talked for a minute and Tom nodded. Then, Billy looked across the room and tipped his hat to Maxwell's men.

When the next polka started, Billy come over and asked me if he could dance with Susan. I agreed. As he spun her quickly around the floor, Susan looked happy to be with the best dancer at the baile. They were laughing as he brought her back to her seat and thanked me.

Three times during the evening, Billy danced with Delvina Maxwell. She was a Navaho woman who had been captured by the Utes as a young girl. She was freed from her captors when Lucian Maxwell traded a horse for her. Since that time, she had worked as a servant for the Maxwell family. She was a short woman, nearly as wide as she was tall. She was very homely, but there was kindness in her face.

Billy deliberately slowed down his gait so she could follow him with her choppy steps. He would waltz her about and stare at her with a big grin. She did her best to follow his steps while she smiled and looked up at him. I wondered if the little Navaho woman had ever enjoyed that kind of attention in her life.

The dance finally broke up about midnight.

While we were getting into our buggy, Billy came over to see us off. He thanked us for coming and looked forward to visiting us after everything cooled down. This was a much more confidant boy than we had met less than a year earlier.

He said that he and his friends would be going up the Pecos to sell their herd of horses. They would follow Uncle John up to the Texas Panhandle so his cowhands could help provide cover for them. When they got back, they would return to Lincoln to help move Manuela Bowdre and Doc Spulock's family to Fort Sumner. Pete Maxwell had offered each of them a job on his ranch.

I asked him if he had considered leaving the territory for good. He said that Fort Sumner felt like home. He got on with all the folks and it was out of the jurisdiction of Lincoln County. The sheriff in Las Vegas had plenty to keep him busy and had little interest in the goings on at Fort Sumner. He explained that Jessie Evans had skinned out for Texas. Murphy and Dolan were finished. McSween was dead and Chisum was moving his operation to Texas.

We told him to be careful.

He laughed and went to join his pals.

16

With the Regulators out of town, Fort Sumner again became quiet and uneventful. Susan decided to keep her makeshift school going through the summer. The children and their parents were happy with this arrangement. We never wanted for food in those days. The mothers would send something home with Susan nearly every day.

We received two letters on the same day. The first was from Harold Early. He was enjoying his new role as managing editor of the Daily Optic. He had bought a small home in Las Vegas. He joked that his biggest obstacle was keeping his new found power from going to his head. He had proposed to Luisa. They were set to be married in late September.

The letter from Chicago was not welcomed news. Danny had been knocked out in a prizefight. He had spent six days in the hospital until he had regained all his mental faculties. Our family and his friends were pleading with him to quit the ring. My guess was that he would not quit. Prize fighting had become his identity. He thrived on the attention that he received all over Chicago.

When the Regulators returned from Lincoln, they brought Charley Bowdre's wife, Manuela, with them along with Doc Spurloc's wife and children. They also had a herd of about a hundred and fifty cattle that they had stolen from the Charles Fritz ranch, near Carrizozo. Stealing livestock back and forth seemed to be the primary form of commerce in New Mexico Territory.

The papers carried stories about the removal of Governor Axtell by President Hayes. Axtell was nothing more than an incompetent tool of Thomas Catron. Former Union General Lew Wallace would replace him. Wallace had presided over the conspiracy trial in the murder of Abraham Lincoln and he had recently published a book called, BEN HURR. The new governor would not be pushed around by Boss Catron. It appeared that things were finally moving in the right direction in New Mexico.

No sooner had the Regulators settled Manuela Bowdre and the Spurlock family in the old Indian hospital at Fort Sumner, than they left for Tascosa, on the Texas Panhandle. This lawless town was known as a market for stolen livestock. Buyers beware with no questions asked.

In early November, only Billy and Tom O'Folliard returned from Tascosa. They brought along a new friend named Henry Hoyt. They had met him on the way to Texas. Billy and Henry had become fast friends. Dr. Hoyt had graduated from medical school in St. Louis. He had come west looking for adventure.

When the Billy and the others were ready to leave Tascosa, Fred Waite decided to return to his family in Oklahoma. Henry Brown left for Kansas. John Middleton figured he would stay in Texas and get work with one of the large ranches on the Panhandle.

Several days later, Henry Hoyt stopped by the post office on his way to Las Vegas. He was a small man who wore a frock coat and a derby hat. He had a friendly smile and an intelligent look about him. I asked him to come in and sit down. I wanted to hear about the trip to Tascosa.

When I asked Henry about his two months with the Regulators, he was happy to explain. He said that he had met them on the trail to Tascosa. At first, he worried about falling in with a group of cattle rustlers. In those days, a man might be killed for his horse and saddle. After listening to Billy explain his philosophy and sing a few songs, Hoyt knew he was in no danger.

Henry described the two months he had spent camped in a grove of cottonwoods on the south edge of Tascosa. He thought that Billy and Tom O'Folliard were like brothers. They both had quick minds and a fine sense of humor. He said that Billy was clearly the leader of the group.

Hoyt described a situation that had occurred at the Howard and McMasters Store, where the group would spend the day playing cards. He said O'Folliard had gotten into a disagreement with a local gambler and the two men were about to draw their weapons. Billy stepped in and pulled O'Folliard off to the side. He talked quietly to O'Folliard until the red head had calmed down. Hoyt was struck with Billy's presence of mind, being only eighteen years of age.

Henry told of another tense moment when the boys were ready to move some of their livestock. John Middleton had been drinking and was in the middle of a card game. He said Middleton was a fearless looking man who gave no quarter to anyone. He thought that Middleton was the most menacing individual among the Regulators.

Billy approached the table and told Middleton that he needed his help. Middleton shook his head, no. Billy repeated that he needed his help, but Middleton said he wasn't leaving the game. You're coming with us, Billy said as his hand went down to his gun. Billy said that he would wait outside for him. Middleton reluctantly cashed out and joined the others.

The most interesting story that Hoyt had to offer was when legendary lawman Bat Masterson came to Tascosa. He was introduced to Billy and the others. Masterson spent several days playing cards with the group. There was nothing but good humor and agreeable conversation. Henry said that it was easy to see why Masterson was so well liked. He had an air of humility. His attitude was never aloof or superior in any way.

One morning, it was suggested that Billy and Masterson should have a shooting contest. Someone was sent to the local trash heap to gather cans and bottles. Eight bottles were set on fence posts, maybe fifty yards away. In turn, Billy and Bat drew their pistols and hit all four of their targets.

It was decided that more difficulty was required. A man, about twenty yards away, would throw a can into the air. Each man would have to draw his gun and shoot. Ten cans were thrown into the air. If a can wasn't hit on the first shot, it was hit on the second. The difference was that Billy was quicker to fire. He would hit the can at the top of its arc when it was almost stationary. Masterson had the more difficult task of hitting the can on its downward trajectory.

Henry was anxious to relate another story. He said that he had won a woman's gold pocket watch in a card game. Billy asked to look at the fancy timepiece. He was so impressed with the watch that Henry decided to make Billy a gift of it. Billy said he couldn't take the watch, but Henry insisted.

Hoyt said that Billy marched over to the counter and scratched out a note with a pencil. At this point, Henry pulled a folded piece of paper out of his pocket and handed it to me. It read:

Tascosa, Texas

Thursday Oct 24th, 1878

*Know all persons by these presents
that I hereby sell and deliver
to Henry F. Hoyt one Sorrell
Horse Branded BB on left hip
and other indistinct Branded on
Shoulders for the sum of seventy five
dollars in hand received.*

W.H. Bonney

*Witness
Jas E. McMasters
Geo. J. Howard*

I looked out the door. Sure enough, there was the nice looking sorrel gelding that Billy had been riding when he had stopped by the post office earlier that summer. I decided not to mention that the horse once belonged to Sheriff Brady and Billy had stolen it to settle a score.

Henry said that it was time for him to leave for Las Vegas. I shook hands and said goodbye to the likable young man. I suggested that he look up my good friend, Harold Early, when he reached town. I thought Harold might help him find some kind of decent work.

17

One year after the murder of John Tunstall, five of the Regulators, including Billy Bonney, Doc Spurlock, Tom O'Folliard, George Bowers and Yginio Salazar, left Fort Sumner for Lincoln. They hoped to take advantage of Lew Wallace's offer of amnesty for participants in the Lincoln County War. They may not have been aware that the offer did not apply to anyone with existing warrants.

When the five men reached Lincoln, they were told that Jesse Evans and his gang were also in town. Billy sent a messenger to propose a truce between the two factions. Put the killing behind them. The messenger reported back that Evans and his men would take the south side of the street and Billy's men could line up on the north side.

With both factions behind protective walls, Jesse Evans hollered that he would kill Billy Bonney on sight.

Billy called back that he would prefer not to open the negotiations with a fight, but if they would come at him three at a time, he would whip the whole bunch of them.

The two sides slowly came out from behind their protective walls and repaired to a saloon where the details of a treaty could be worked out. The meeting went late into the night. A great deal of whiskey was consumed. Finally, the meeting broke up and the men left the saloon.

Outside, they encountered a one armed lawyer named Houston Chapman. He had been hired by Susan McSween to bring a case against Colonel Dudley in the wrongful death of Alexander McSween. Jesse Campbell, of the Evans gang, had recently met with Colonel Dudley to discuss the problem that Chapman might cause for him.

Lawyer Chapman crossed the street in front of the drunken mob. Jesse Campbell fired a shot at Chapman's feet and ordered him to dance. When Chapman refused, Campbell shot the lawyer in the chest. Jimmy Dolan then put another slug in Chapman while he lay on the ground.

Dolan insisted that they all go back into the saloon and discuss the matter. Campbell boasted that he had promised God and Colonel Dudley that he would kill Chapman and now it was done. Dolan realized that a gun would have to be planted on Chapman. Billy, who had not been drinking, said he would plant the weapon.

Once outside, Billy confided to his friends that he had no intention of planting the gun on the dead lawyer. Let Jimmy Dolan explain what had happened. The five men collected their horses and rode east to San Patricio. The next morning, Chapman was found unarmed.

Several weeks later, Billy heard that Governor Lew Wallace was on his way to Lincoln to open an inquiry into the violence in Lincoln County. Billy wrote a letter to Wallace offering his testimony concerning the death of Houston Chapman. In return, he asked that Wallace might help him with his existing indictments.

A few days later, Billy received a reply from Wallace. He asked Billy to meet him at nine o'clock on the night of March 17 at the home of The Justice of the Peace, John Wilson. He said he was willing to discuss Billy's proposal.

When Billy arrived at Wilson's one room home shortly after dark, he had a revolver in one hand and his Winchester in the other. Lew Wallace stood up and introduced himself. When Billy realized that he was in no danger, he set his weapons aside. The two men began to talk.

Wallace explained his proposal. Billy would submit to arrest and be forced to testify before two grand juries concerning the Houston Chapman murder and the malfeasance of Colonel Dudley during the five day siege in Lincoln. Billy agreed to consider the offer and reply within two days,

The two men talked past midnight. Billy attempted to explain the lead up to the Lincoln County War. Wallace took notes while Billy explained the extent of political corruption in the territory.

Billy rode back to San Patricio late that night. The next day, he heard that Jesse Evans and Billy Campbell had escaped from the stockade at Fort Stanton and were on their way to Texas. Billy immediately sent a letter to Wallace and asked if their agreement was still valid.

Wallace assured Billy that if he would testify before the two grand juries, he would issue a full pardon for all of Billy's current indictments. With the opportunity to put his legal problems behind him, Billy agreed to allow himself to be arrested at San Patricio and taken back to Lincoln. Tom O'Folliard, who was also a witness to the Chapman murder, submitted to arrest and went along with Billy.

When Billy and Tom were thrown into the pit that served as a jail in Lincoln, Billy sent word to Governor Wallace that he and Tom might not live long enough to testify. On orders from the governor, the two prisoners were taken to the Juan Patron house in shackles.

While held in custody at the Patron house, the two prisoners were allowed to keep their weapons as protection against a possible attack by Dolan's men. The Mexican people brought them food and cigars. In the evening, guitar players would serenade the two desperados.

To show good faith, Governor Wallace paid a visit to the Patron house before he returned to Santa Fe. He asked if his key witness would be willing wander over to the river for an exhibition of his shooting skills. The former Union general evidently had a level of comfort with his young prisoner. After all, they were fellow travelers from Indiana.

Billy was only too happy to put on a full show. He fired under the neck of his horse while riding at a full gallop. He shot bottles off fence posts. He slapped leather and shot cans out of the air. After Billy had gone through his entire bag of tricks, the governor and the gun fighter returned to the Patron house.

Wallace asked Billy if there was a secret to his accuracy. Billy explained that when a man points with his index finger, he did so with unerring aim. When you point your revolver, he told Wallace, think of the barrel as your index finger and the bullet will always find its mark. Billy failed to mention the thousands of cartridges he had used for practice.

When Wallace returned to Santa Fe, Billy was in fine spirits. He was certain that he had made an important friend. Wallace would make good on his promise. The trick was to stay alive in Lincoln until he could deliver his testimony.

Two months later, Billy had finished his testimony to the grand jury inquiries into the murder of Houston Chapman and the conduct of Colonel Dudley. There was a problem. District Attorney William Rynerson emphatically refused to drop any of the current charges against William Bonney. Rynerson had also won a change of venue from Lincoln to Mesilla. To submit to trial and sentencing and then hope for a pardon from Wallace was too great a risk.

Three weeks later, after three months of incarceration at the Patron house in Lincoln, Billy and Tom O'Folliard said goodbye to their guards. They walked to the corral and saddled their horses. Without fanfare, the two friends rode out of Lincoln.

As Billy rode out of the Rio Bonito Valley, he knew it was unlikely that he would ever receive the pardon that had been promised by Lew Wallace. By testifying before the two grand juries, he had set himself up to be shot in the back by any of Jimmy Dolan's men. From here on, Billy would survive outside the law.

18

The New Mexico & Southern Pacific railhead was due to reach Las Vegas on Independence Day, 1879. Billy and Tom O'Folliard decided to take part in the big celebration and the rampant gambling. They had been at Fort Sumner for less than a month.

The chance to wreak havoc on a once sleepy town was not lost on a number of desperate types from Dodge City, Kansas. Doc Holiday, Dave Mather, Hoodoo Brown, Joe Carson, Dave Rudabaugh and Tom Pickett were on their way. Hoodoo Brown was soon elected as Justice of the Peace. He appointed Dave Rudabaugh and Tom Pickett to the police force. This allowed the lawless element from Dodge City to take control of Las Vegas.

After he had been in Las Vegas for several weeks, Billy encountered his old friend, Henry Hoyt. Billy asked Henry to join him for dinner at the Adobe Hotel at Hot Springs with a new acquaintance named, Mr. Howard. After the meal, Billy told Hoyt that Mr. Howard was actually Jesse James. Billy had met him two days earlier during a game of Monte.

Billy said that James had come to New Mexico to scout out the railroad situation as well as a possible place to move his family. The previous day, James had asked Billy to return to Missouri with him and join a new gang that he was organizing. Billy declined. He told James that robbing banks and trains was not his chosen line of work.

Six weeks after the railhead reached Las Vegas, gold was discovered at White Oaks. This was a small town, high in the mountains, north of Lincoln and west of Fort Sumner. Billy and his friends decided to vacate Las Vegas and head for White Oaks. There was always loose money in a new mining town.

With hundreds of new miners arriving in White Oaks, there was a great demand for beef. Billy realized after the Las Vegas experience that gambling was no sure way to make a living. He had run his own Monte game for a time. The odds were strongly on the side of the dealer, but a bad run had used up his limited capital.

Billy still held a grudge against John Chisum for not compensating the Regulators for guarding the McSweens on their return to Lincoln. Several of Billy's friends were killed in the five day standoff. When Billy and Chisum parted company on the way to Texas, Billy told him that if he refused to make good on his promise, Billy would help himself to Chisum's cattle.

Billy came up with a plan to steal cattle from Chisum and sell the livestock in White Oaks or Las Vegas. He had found a natural holding pen in a canyon at The Portales. They would poach cows from the edges of the great herd until they had a sufficient number to drive to market.

While in White Oaks, Billy made the acquaintance of Whiskey Jim Greathouse, who had a stage stop and ranch west of the new mining town. Greathouse had gotten his nickname during his years in Texas when he made a fine profit selling redeye to the Indians. Greathouse made it clear to Billy that he would not ask too many questions about cattle that were moved onto his ranch, so long as he saw a piece of the action.

Billy was always on the move that summer

between Portales, White oaks and Fort Sumner. He would stay with Charlie Bowdre at the old Indian hospital or he would bunk with one of his Hispano friends in town. He had the air of busy cattleman who was trying to keep up with the great demand for his product.

When Billy was at Fort Sumner, he and Pat Garrett became regular gambling pals. They were seen together so often that folks began to call them Little Casino and Big Casino. Garrett was deadly serious about cards. Billy did not appear to be serious about anything. He would often give his last ten dollars to a friend.

Susan and I saw very little of Billy that summer. He would occasionally stop by to see what was being written about him in the newspapers, but he wouldn't stay long. I could never get him to stay for supper as he always had a girl waiting for him at Sumner. He seemed to know every woman in town and was equally fond of all of them.

On one visit to the post office, Billy told me that he had learned that Bob Olinger had killed his good friend, John Jones. Jones had been shot four times in the back. Billy said that he had ridden down to Seven Rivers to offer his condolences to the Jones family. He warned the younger Jones boys not to confront Olinger or they might be killed. Billy promised the family that he would take care of Olinger.

19

The August weather had turned very hot. The heat was interrupted only by occasional thundershowers. All I could think of was drinking a few beers at Bob Hargrove's Saloon at Fort Sumner. I told Susan that I had to go by the blacksmith's and headed off to town.

When I reached the saloon, I found Billy seated against the wall with his chair tilted back and his boots on the table. He was staring at the bar where a burly fellow was talking loudly to no one in particular.

"He reminds me of Cahill," Billy stared at the man.

Cahill was the blacksmith that Billy had killed at Fort Grant. Even though Cahill was dead, Billy still seemed to harbor a grudge against the man. The stranger at the bar looked like a miner, possibly from White Oaks. He stood about six feet tall. His arms were the size of a keg of nails.

"He's been in here two hours and he won't shut up," Billy continued to stare at the big man. The miner was unarmed so Billy couldn't let his anger get him into trouble.

The miner turned and announced in a German accent to the eight of us in the saloon, "I'll whip every sissy in this room at the same time. With these two hands." I could tell by his words that he was liquored to the gills.

"That's enough," Billy muttered. "Give it a rest," he called out.

The miner pushed off from the bar and walked to our table. Billy's hand went down to his gun.

"You two little runts want to dance?" He stared across the table at us.

"Go get your gun, mister," Billy suggested.

"I don't have no need for no gun," The man leaned forward. "I have these," he grinned as he raised his two hands. Either hand would reach all the way around a man's neck. I could smell his foul breath across the table.

"Get on back, you damned blowhard," Billy warned.

"No need for that gun, boy," the miner

smiled. "You two darlings wanna dance?"

My anger finally kicked in, "It won't take two of us, you drunken bastard. I'm the one who's going to teach you some manners," I said as I stood up.

"Well, let's go then, sonny" The big man's eyes were wide as he turned toward the door. My only thought was not to let him get ahold of me with one of those huge hands. As we left the saloon, Billy followed us. He looked excited.

The first thing I made certain was to keep some distance between us and stay clear of the building. As I expected, he came at me in a rush. He threw a clumsy right hand. I stepped to the left and hit him on the side of the face with a hard right hand. The punch had no effect on him.

He rushed at me again. This time I stepped out of the way to the right and landed a hard right to his chin as he went by. Still no damage. He lunged by me two more times as I landed hard punches to his head.

The fifth time he charged, I ducked and stepped to the left. With all of my weight behind it, I buried a right uppercut to the center of his gut. This had the proper effect. He fell to his knees and gasped for air.

I knew this was my best chance to finish him.

As he rose to his feet with his hands holding his stomach, I hit him four times in the head. He would not go down.

I moved around to his left side and beat his rib cage with everything I had. When his hands went down to guard his ribs, I threw three punches to his face. The last punch caught him on the point of the chin. He went down face forward, with his arms at his side.

I stood over him and watched his mouth drooling blood onto the dirt. I waited for the miner to rise. My hands were sore from the blows to his head. I was relieved when he did not get up.

Billy put his hand on my shoulder, "I'll buy every drop you can drink, damn you." He was as excited as I had ever seen him.

When we got inside, Billy ordered drinks all around. As the others came through the door, they slapped me on the back.

"Good show."

"Knuckle to skull, by God."

"The loudmouth got what was coming."

"You want whiskey," Billy asked. He guided me to a chair as if he were my corner man.

Billy ordered whiskey for the crowd and a beer for both of us. He was grinning from ear to ear. Those two front teeth were never more evident. He turned and announced to the others, "This is Robert O'Dell. He will not stand by for that kind of blowhardry and neither will I."

The whole crowd was in loud conversation as they relived the event that had taken place outside. "Robert O'Dell," they would toast the hero of the moment with their free drinks held high.

"That was something," Billy shook his head. "If I live to be fifty, I may never see anything like it."

I threw down the beer. Billy called for another. I didn't feel the need to remind the celebrants that the big German was already drunk. I kept watching the door. The last thing I wanted was to see that angry bear of a man rush toward me. No clever fisticuffs would save me if he ever got ahold of me.

The big miner must have decided to be on his way. That suited me fine. Billy and I kept drinking beer until the saloon had become quiet. I told him that I had better get back to Sunnyside.

"This is a celebration," Billy protested. "You should stay awhile."

"No," I said. "As much as I'd like to stay here and soak up the glory, Susan is already wondering where I am."

"I'll abide by that, Robert. We want to stay on her good side. I'll see you off. You look a little wobbly," he laughed.

As we walked out of Hargrove's saloon, we could hear a horse screaming. Fifty yards to our left, I saw a man holding a roan filly by the reins and quirting her about the head.

Billy pulled out his revolver. He fired a shot into the air as we walked toward the man. He stopped the beating his horse. As he turned to face us, the filly wheeled and tried to get loose.

Billy fought to seize the reins from the man, who I knew as Ben Wiggins. When the man pushed Billy away, Billy brought the barrel of his gun against his chest. Billy took hold of the reins and led the filly a few feet away.

"What the hell." Wiggins yelled.

"Give me two reasons or even one, why I shouldn't plant you right here," Billy pointed his revolver at the man.

"That's my horse," Wiggins complained.

"Not anymore, she's not." Billy kept his revolver leveled at the man as he handed the reins to me. A crowd had started to gather. This was not lost on Billy.

"I'll give you one hour to get out of town," Billy said. He was now playing to the bystanders. "If I see you here after that, your prospects will not be cheerful."

"You can't take a man's horse," Wiggins whined.

"I just did. Every minute you stand here puts you one step closer to the bone yard."

Wiggins looked at Billy's gun and walked back a few steps. "What about my saddle?'

"You ever heard of forfeiture?"

"What's forfeiture?"

"That's this," I could see that Billy's anger had gone down a notch. He was amused by his own remark.

"Well, damn," Wiggins muttered as he walked away.

Billy enjoyed the attention as we walked toward the stable with the small filly. No one in these parts would dare cross Billy. He knew that. He had rescued an abused filly. That pleased him. I was certain that all of his admirers in town would be anxious to tell the tale.

"You and I are a lot the same, "Billy commented as we walked. "Neither of us will tolerate that sort of thing."

"It worked out pretty well, today," I agreed. "Are you going to give Wiggins his horse back?"

"I expect I'll have to," Billy sounded

reluctant. "But he better pray I don't see him beating this filly again."

"I'd say you've given him fair warning."

"More than fair, Robert. More than fair."

"That's good enough."

"I'll never forget the way you danced around that big blowhard," Billy didn't want to let it go. "The way you landed all those blows without getting touched."

"The next fella may not be drunk."

"No," Billy pressed on. "The outcome would have been no different. I feel the same way when I step in. The other fella has no good prospect."

"Speaking for myself, I'd rather not do this every week."

"That's true enough," Billy nodded. "But some of these lousy bastards don't give you any selection."

20

On a peaceful Sunday morning in late October, Susan and I decided to try our luck at the best fishing hole this side of Fort Sumner. Lonesome Joe led the way. As soon as I picked up the jar of grasshoppers, Joe was on his way to the river. We followed a trail for two hundred yards through the greasewood and prickly pear.

With little effort, Susan caught three good sized trout in half an hour. When I glanced at her string of fish, her expression was one of complete superiority. This was fine by me. I encouraged her vanities so long as I could crawl under the quilt with her every night. I really had no ambition other than being married to Susan O'Dell. The former Susan Finnegan. The most fetching girl on the north side of Chicago.

"Oh, Winston," she smiled.

"Yes, Milady," I dutifully walked along the bank toward her.

"I will have you clean these fish now." She handed me the string of trout.

"Oh yes, Milady," I bowed as I accepted the string of fish. "Would there be anything else?"

"Yes, Winston," she said with her nose in the air. "When you're finished, scrub up properly and see me in my chambers." she turned and walked toward the house. I watched as she swung her hips in saloon fashion.

With haste, I cleaned the three fish. It would be safe to wager that I did scrub up properly. When I walked in the front door, I called out, "I'm here, Milady."

Susan answered from the bedroom, "Don't dally, Winston."

Later, after I had obeyed every whim of Milady, we sipped our coffee and ate breakfast. Along with the trout, we had a stack of hotcakes with chokecherry jam. A man could ask for nothing more than the bounty I had received on Sunday morning. As we finished our coffee, we decided to take the buggy into Sumner and watch a much-anticipated horse race.

Pete Maxwell had bought a strapping chestnut stallion from Mexico. He wanted to upgrade the quality of his herd of horses. Pete was confident that he had acquired an animal that could outrun Billy's exceptional bay mare. This match race had been the topic of conversation around town for the past week.

Racing horses was a Sunday tradition in all the placitas along the Pecos. A stretch of road below Fort Sumner ran south along the river for just over half a mile until it turned east. Maxwell wanted a shorter race, but Billy had insisted that the bend in the road should be the finish line.

We rode past the fort until we saw a crowd of people gathered at the race's starting point. It was not yet noon, but it appeared that everyone in the settlement had turned out for the event. Folks were lined up for fifty yards along the west side of the road.

A young vaquero, maybe fifteen years old, who worked for Maxwell, sat on the chestnut horse. The boy had been chosen because of his size. He could not have weighed more than a hundred pounds. The Maxwell stallion was impressive. His coat had a bright copper sheen and his massive hind quarters rippled with power. He was on the muscle as he toe danced on the road.

Pete Maxwell mingled with the Mexicans

who worked for him. They looked confident as they laughed and watched the powerful animal. I was sure that a considerable amount of money had been wagered on the Mexican invader.

On the other side of the road were Billy's supporters. Charley and Manuela Bowdre were laughing with Tom O'Folliard and Barney Mason. Bob Hargrove and Beaver Smith were on hand. They had closed their saloons to watch the race. They were confident that Billy's tall bay mare would prevail.

Paulita Maxwell stood by herself and watched Billy on his light-footed bay. The well-balanced horse looked relaxed as Billy stroked her neck and positioned her for the start.

Pat Garret would start the race. He had a red bandana in his right hand. The race would start when he dropped his right arm. He had a serious expression that had become his trademark since he had wandered into Fort Sumner.

"I won't ask who your money's with, Pat," Billy grinned as he settled his horse.

"Never mind about that," Garrett looked up at him. "You just get to that corner first."

"You'll give us a square start, won't you, Pat," Billy was in his moment with the large crowd watching his every move. He knew how close Garrett was with his money and he was having some fun with him.

"You ready?" Garrett looked tense. "Listo?" he asked the young Mexican rider.

The boy nodded and Garrett dropped his arm.

The muscled chestnut exploded down the road. He was unbelievably quick as he reached full gallop in four or five strides.

"Can I go, Pat?" Billy looked down at Garret.

"Go, damn you," Garrett yelled.

Billy shook the reins and his bay was off. It took her longer to gain her full stride, but she covered the ground with long smooth strides. Her hooves appeared to barely flick the sandy ground. At full gallop, she took one stride for every two of the chestnut stallion.

"Damn that kid," Garrett muttered.

It looked like the Billy had given the Mexican horse too much of an advantage. He was still about a hundred yards behind as they hit the halfway point of the race. The thought crossed my mind that Billy might have bet on the other horse.

From where we stood, you could see the dust of the smaller horse quite a ways ahead of the bay mare. Maxwell's cowhands were whopping it up. The celebration had begun.

On the other side of the road, there was a look of concern. There were no smiles among Billy's supporters. "Crooked son-of-a-bitch," Barney Mason said what some of the others were probably thinking.

As the two horses were about three quarters of the way to the bend, you could see the dust from Billy's mare begin to narrow the margin. It was difficult to see the animals, but the dust had narrowed. As the two horses got closer to the turn, the tall mare inhaled the smaller colt and pulled away.

Pat Garrett threw his head back and laughed. Spanish swear words could be heard on the other side of the road. Billy knew exactly what he had in his horse, but he wanted to create the maximum excitement. He was the ultimate showman.

A few minutes later, when the two horses trotted back to the crowd, the Mexican people greeted the young vaquero with sympathy. They knew he had given the colt a great start and a good ride. They even cheered El Chivato. He had made it a good show.

"Pat, you have the look of a fella whose wealthy uncle just passed on," Billy smiled.

"Damn you, Billy," Garrett laughed as he patted him on the leg. "I'm not going to get scooped into another deal like this again."

"I believe I'll accept that beer you were intending to buy me," Billy joked.

"You should by me a drink after that stunt." Garrett said as he walked away.

Billy stayed mounted on his tall mare and gazed about the friendly crowd. As the chestnut colt was led away, Billy smiled at his admirers. This day belonged to him.

21

As the calendar turned to 1880, everything was quiet at Sunnyside. Winter meant fewer travelers on the road. I kept the fire stoked in the post office and in our small adobe across the road. There was not much else to do. On Saturday afternoon, I decided to ride into town for a beer.

When I arrived at Bob Hargrove's saloon, there were only three patrons on hand. I took a seat at a table along side Charlie Bowdre. He looked bored as he stared at a tall man who stood against the bar.

"Says he's from Texas," Charlie explained. "Joe Grant's his name. Fancies himself as Texas Red. He's been tossing down whiskey all day."

I looked across the room at the stranger. He had red hair and freckles. His eyes had the look of a man who hadn't slept in a few days. He was maybe six foot-two and broad shouldered. He had a reddish mustache that went down past his chin. He wore a black hat that was tipped back on his head. His gun was low on his hip as if he considered himself a pistolero.

"Earlier today he tried to bet Billy that he would kill a man before Billy would. Billy said, 'Joe, why would you want to kill anybody?' Grant insisted so they each put up five dollars for Hargrove to hold. There's speculation that Grant has come here to kill Billy. Word is he worked for Chisum."

"Where's Billy now?"

"He's out at the cow camp. Jim Chisum came through here rounding up strays and rebrands. Billy went out with him to make sure he only took back his own stock. Jim and Billy have always got along well. Will Chisum and Billy are fishing partners at South Springs. And you know Billy always has some kind of present or other for Sally when he's down there."

"He's sweet on Sally, isn't he?"

Bowdre smiled, "He's sweet on all of 'em."

I sat back and sipped my beer while I watched Joe Grant. The bottom of his tan trousers was tucked inside a pair of high black boots. He might be considered a threat to Billy if you didn't know Billy. The big man nursed his whiskey and stared at his image in the mirror behind the bar.

There had been a similar situation a few months previous. Another Texan, by the name of Jack Long, had arrived from Fort Griffin. Word was out that he had killed a man there and was on the run. Apparently, his intention was to shoot up Fort Sumner and terrorize the local folks. The nearest law was more than a hundred miles north at Las Vegas.

Long was liquored up and firing his pistol in the street when Billy walked out of the dry goods store. He heard the shooting and jumped behind a post for protection.

"Come out, buddy," Jack Long hollered from the parade grounds. "I won't shoot you."

"The hell you won't," Billy answered. "There's no danger of you hurting anyone unless it's by accident." Then, Billy made reference to the rumored killing at Fort Griffin, "They say you kill all your men by accident."

Long stared across the street at Billy, "Where are you from, buddy?"

"Every place on earth except this," Billy mocked the bad man.

The next day, Long was holding court with three other strangers at Beaver Smith's saloon.

Billy walked in with Charley Payne. They took a seat in the rear of the room.

Long yelled at Billy, "Where do you think you're going, you damn little bastard?"

Billy stood up and walked over to Long. In a quiet voice, he asked, "Who did you address that remark to, sir?"

"I was joking with that other fellow," Long said.

Billy looked at Long, "Be very careful when you joke with fellows in whose company I happen to be. Perhaps I'm too stupid to understand your jokes. If you ever drop another one that hits the ground as close to me as that last one did, I'll crack your crust. Do you understand?"

Billy walked back to his chair. Jack Long left town the next morning.

I ordered a second beer. Bowdre said that Joe Grant had been hurling insults at no one in particular all afternoon. If Billy were on hand, Grant might not get off as easily as Jack Long did.

Charley wasn't in much of a mood for conversation. I sipped my beer and watched the blustering giant from Texas.

I was about to leave when a group of six men entered the saloon. There were three men I didn't know followed by Charley Thomas, Barney Mason and Billy. The Kid gave Charlie and me a big smile as he sat down at a table with the others.

As the men began to drink a round of whiskey, Joe Grant walked over to the table and pulled a pearl handled revolver out of one man's holster. Grant replaced the gun with his own revolver. The man rose to get his gun back, but Billy put his hand on the man's shoulder.

"Take it easy," Billy said.

Billy walked to the bar where Grant was standing. Grant had set the pearl handled revolver on the counter.

"That's a beauty, Red," Billy said as he picked up the firearm. He rotated the cylinder to see if the gun was loaded. He set the gun back on the bar.

Grant picked up the gun and aimed it toward the table where the other five men were sitting. "I'm gonna kill John Chisum," Grant hollered. "The old son-of-a-bitch."

"Hold on there, Red. You've got the wrong pig by the ear"," Billy explained. "That's not John Chisum. That's his brother, Jim."

"You're a goddamn liar," Grant said as Billy turned to walk away.

"Billy," several of us yelled as Grant raised

the fancy revolver and pointed it at the back of Billy's head.

Billy took another step until he heard the hollow click from the hammer falling on an empty chamber. Billy whirled to his left as he drew his gun and fired three quick shots. Grant fell backwards with his head landing at the far corner of the bar.

Billy walked over and looked down at Grant. He studied the dead man for a moment and said, "I've been there too many times, Red."

Billy went back to the table and sat down to finish his beer. The saloon was silent. Everyone watched Billy as he calmly sipped his beer.

Bob Hargrove asked for help to carry the body outside. He didn't want Grant to bleed out on the plank floor. Charley and I got up along with the cowhand whose pearl handled revolver now lay on the floor.

When we reached the body, I could see three bullet wounds in Grant's chin. All three bullet holes were within the arc of the red mustache. The back of Grant's head was blasted out. The Chisum man picked up his gun and dropped Grant's revolver on the floor. Grant must have weighed two hundred and fifty pounds as we dragged him out the door.

Later, whenever anyone asked Billy about the fight with Joe Grant, Billy would say, "It was a game of two and I got there first," or, "His gun wouldn't work and mine would." Always the clever remark. Always the showman.

The killing of Joe Grant proved to me that the incident at Puerto de Luna was no bluff. Billy was fast and sure. Unlike most men, he was completely calm when the stakes were the highest. Unlike anyone I had ever known, Billy seemed to have no concern for mortality.

22

Four days after the death of Joe Grant, Billy, Tom O'Folliard and Charley Bowdre attended Pat Garrett's wedding in Anton Chico. They had ridden eighty miles up the Pecos to give their friend a proper send off. While Garrett married Apolonaria Gutiérrez, Barney Mason married Juanita Madril. The weddings were followed by a dance, which attracted all the Mexican girls for miles around. This may have been the primary reason that Billy and his friends had made the long trip to Anton Chico.

Later in the year, the three pals made a trip to Lincoln when Susan McSween married a man named George Barber. It seemed that no distance was too great if there was a wedding celebration. If the lawmen that dogged Billy throughout the year of 1880 really wanted to catch the young outlaw, they would only have to find the nearest dance. Find the baile and you would likely find Billy.

A problem was beginning to take shape. Most of Billy's friends had left the territory. Charley Bowdre and Tom O'Folliard had taken jobs on the Yerby ranch, north of Fort Sumner. Billy could not consider a permanent job at one of these ranches. He could not afford to be a stationary target for U.S. Marshalls, cattle detectives or back shooters. Billy had to remain on the dodge.

Another problem had occurred with the death of Joe Grant. It was the second man that Billy had killed, outside of the gun battles that had taken place during the Lincoln County War. As with the blacksmith at Fort Grant, Billy could easily claim self defense in both of these killings. The problem was, in the territorial papers and in the minds of the authorities, Joe Grant's death enhanced Billy's reputation as a killer.

When Billy ran out of money, his solution was to organize a small band of rustlers to poach cattle from the big outfits on the Texas Panhandle. His primary target was John Chisum, but he did not ignore the other large spreads. They would rebrand the cattle and take them to the boomtowns of Las Vegas or White Oaks where there was a great demand for beef.

Billy would then lay low at Fort Sumner or one of the placitas in the area until his money ran out. Billy didn't care much about money except having enough for gambling. To gather men to help move stolen beeves, Billy wound up traveling with some noted outlaws. These wanted criminals were clearly a step down from the small ranchers that Billy had ridden with during the fight in Lincoln.

Billy Wilson was wanted for passing counterfeit money. Wilson had sold his livery stable in White Oaks and may have been paid in bogus money. The problem for Wilson was that the government in Washington had sent an agent to track Wilson. Billy Bonney's new friend was wanted for a federal offense.

Justice of the Peace Hoodoo Brown had appointed Dave Rudabaugh and Tom Pickett to the police force in Las Vegas. Brown had used these two men and others to rob stagecoaches and commit other criminal acts. Rudabaugh was wanted in Las Vegas for killing a deputy sheriff while breaking Joe Webb out of jail. These were the kind of men who partnered with Billy to steal cattle.

The big cattle outfits were getting tired of losing thirty or forty head of cows at a time. They hired cattle detectives to comb New Mexico Territory in search of the stolen cattle. When the thieves were identified, the ranches would send out groups of men to look for the culprits. These became known as "panhandle posses".

Billy was often in Fort Sumner, but only for a few days at a time. When any of his friends would suggest that the authorities were closing in on him, Billy would disappear. He had little respect for those who were chasing him, but he couldn't allow himself to be caught by surprise.

In the fall of 1880, Pat Garrett decided to move to Roswell. He had been encouraged by Joseph Lea and John Chisum to run for sheriff in Lincoln County. In order to win that post, he had to be a resident of the county. The current sheriff in Lincoln, George Kimbrell, was a friend of Billy's. The cattlemen were looking for a man who would put a stop to the theft of their livestock.

On a Saturday in early October, Garrett loaded a wagon and prepared for the trip to Roswell. A handful of us went out to the road to see him off.

"Well, Pat," Billy said as he stood next to the

wagon, "If you win this thing, I expect you'll be coming after me."

Garrett sat with the reins in his hands. His wife stared ahead. I wasn't sure if Apolonaria knew much English.

"You know, Billy," Garrett said slowly, "The days of you free riders has about ended. Jesse Evans is serving a life sentence in the Texas State Penitentiary. Most of your pals have left the territory. It might be time for you to consider a new line of work."

"Well." Billy explained, "You know we just work the edges of those herds. Chisum still owes me money. The big outfits on the Panhandle don't even know where their strays have wandered."

"That's well and good, Billy, but they mean to put an end to losing those beeves. Your best bet would be to head for Colorado. Or better yet, California. Get a clean start."

"You may be right, Pat, but all my good friends are here along the Pecos. I worry about what the bailes might be like in California?"

"All right, Billy." Garrett sounded irritated. "I can see you're not of a mind to leave out of here, but those Texans are looking for you."

"Maybe ol' George will win this election." Billy grinned. "Then we can stay friends."

"I intend to win this election," Garrett looked at Billy.

"All right, Pat," Billy's eyes narrowed. "Good luck to you and Apolonaria."

"Well, adios, boys." Garrett shook the reins and they were off.

23

In late October 1880, I received a small parcel from my sister in Chicago. I had a bad feeling as I opened the package. When I saw Danny's St. Christopher's medallion, I knew that he was dead. I lay the medal and chain on the counter.

My mind raced back to when we were kids. Laughing or fighting. One or the other. But we always stood up for one another. Looking back, it seemed that Danny had been with me every step of the way. Now, I was in New Mexico and Danny was gone.

The letter from Kathleen said that Danny had decided to take one last fight before he quit the ring. It would be his fiftieth bout. He wanted to go out a winner. He was matched with a Polish fighter that he had already beaten. Danny was winning the match until he was hit with a right in the ninth round. When he fell back, he hit his head on the corner post. He was dead when they carried him out of the ring.

Kathleen said they would have a wake for Danny before they buried him next to my mother and my sister. She knew I couldn't be there so she had sent me Danny's St. Christopher medal. He always thought that the medal was all he needed to walk this earth unharmed. Danny was forever the carefree boy who made friends so easily. He reminded me of Billy in many ways.

I had the afternoon to think about Danny before Susan got home from her classroom at Fort Sumner. For the first time, I felt guilty about leaving Chicago. I knew that I couldn't have talked Danny into quitting the ring, anymore than I could talk Billy into leaving the territory. Everyone was drawn to both of those boys because of their friendly nature. In turn, they wanted everyone to like them. They lived to play the crowd.

It had gotten cool late that afternoon. I built a fire in the corner fireplace and waited for Susan. My mind raced over every moment that Danny and I had enjoyed together. Even the fights. Neither one of us would stay angry.

Rolling in the dirt while we clawed at each other was part of what made us close. I suppose most brothers are that way.

When Susan got home and saw the medallion, she knew what had happened. She lit a candle and began to cry. "Poor, poor Danny," was all she could say.

We sat by the fire for a long while. As I stared into the fire, the flames had some kind of meaning. There was life in them that would soon be exhausted. Neither of us thought about supper. To delay the inevitable, I threw two more small logs on the fire. We watched the flames come alive again. Finally, I suggested that we go to bed.

I watched Susan as she sat before the small dresser with an oval mirror. She let down her hair and began to slowly brush out the curls. With the purse from my first prizefight, I had bought her a silver brush and comb with inlaid tortoise shell.

As I watched her in the light from the fire in the next room, I realized how fortunate I was to have quit the fight game and marry Susan. Although she never complained, I thought it was unfair that she should have spent the last three years at this lonely outpost, so far from Chicago.

A week later, we heard that Pat Garrett had

won his election for sheriff in Lincoln County. He had also been appointed as a Deputy U.S. Marshall. This would allow him to search for Billy outside of Lincoln County. The big cattle outfits had found their man. I expected that it would not be long until he rode up the Pecos with a battalion of Texans.

At the end of November, the three newspapers carried stories of a shootout at the Greathouse-Kuch ranch, west of White Oaks. Barney Mason, who was working as an informant for Garrett, had alerted the folks in White Oaks that Billy and several others were in the area. A posse was quickly formed and they caught up with the outlaws at a place called Coyote Springs.

A gun battle ensued. Three of Billy's friends made their escape on horseback, while the Kid and Billy Wilson were forced to escape on foot. The posse may not have wanted to corner Billy in the dark. They collected the belongings from the camp and rode back to White Oaks.

Several days later, another posse of thirteen men managed to corner Bonney, Wilson and Rudabaugh at the Greathouse ranch. When a cook, named Joe Steck, stepped out of the house at daybreak, the posse seized him. They sent him back to the house with a message that the gang must surrender. Billy sent a message back with Steck and asked for someone to discuss the terms.

Jimmy Carlyle, a blacksmith from White Oaks and an acquaintance of Billy's, offered to go in and talk with the outlaws if Jim Greathouse would go outside and stay with the posse. With each side now holding a hostage, a standoff took place for the entire day and into the night. Wilson and Rudabaugh were soaking up free whiskey while Billy tried to plan a way out of the trap.

Billy was confident that his men would outlast the posse. They were warm and well fed inside the house while those outside were dealing with a cold November night. Finally. the posse made it's move. Just before midnight, they sent in a note with Steck. If Jimmy Carlyle wasn't released immediately, the posse would shoot Jim Greathouse. Billy didn't take the threat seriously.

When a frustrated member of the posse fired a shot into the air, Carlisle thought that Greathouse had been killed. He dove through a window onto the snow. He was shot three times. The New Mexican and the Gazette reported that Billy had killed Carlyle. The Optic reported that his own posse had likely shot

Carlyle, as they thought it was one of the outlaws attempting an escape.

The discouraged posse collected the dead body of Jimmy Carlyle and returned to White Oaks. Jim Greathouse, Fred Kuch and the cook saddled their horses and rode to the safety of the nearby Spencer ranch. Billy and his two drunken friends remained at the Greathouse ranch for the night. The following morning they arrived at the Spencer ranch.

The following day, the Greathouse ranch was burned to the ground. Later in the day, the Spencer ranch was burned down. Billy and his two companions had left for parts unknown.

The following week, The Las Vegas Gazette printed a scathing editorial about Billy Bonney. The piece called for an increase in the bounty on "Billy the Kid" from five hundred to five thousand dollars. That's the first time I had heard Billy referred to as "Billy the Kid." In the mind of this editor, Billy was guilty of every wrongdoing that had occurred in the territory since the Lincoln County War.

24

Two days after I had read the Gazette editorial that called for William H. Bonney's head, Billy stepped into the post office. His new habit was to tie his mare behind the building where she couldn't be seen from the road.

"Mornin', Robert," he greeted me with a smile.

"Hello, Billy." I was struck by his relaxed manner.

Billy pulled some papers out of his pocket and laid them on the counter. "One last try with Lew Wallace," he explained. "Take a look. See what you think," he slid the papers in my direction.

I was surprised that Billy was still trying to find favor with Wallace after all that had happened. In part, the letter read:

Fort Sumner
Dec 12th, 1880
Gov. Lew Wallace

Dear Sir,

I noticed in the Las Vegas Gazette a piece which stated that Billy the Kid, the name by which I was known in the country was captain of a Band of Outlaws who hold forth at the Portales. There is no such organization in existence. So the gentleman must have drawn very heavily on his imagination.

Billy went on to explain his version of the death of Jimmy Carlyle at the Greathouse-Kuch ranch.

When I got up the next morning the house was surrounded by an outfit led by one Carlyle who came into the house and demanded a surrender. I asked for papers and they had none. So I concluded that it accounted to nothing more than a mob and told Carlyle that he would have to stay in the house and lead the way out that night. Soon after

a note was brought in stating that if
Carlyle did not come out inside of five
minutes they would kill the station
keeper (Greathouse) who had left the
house and was with them. In a short
time a shot was fired on the outside and
Carlyle thinking Greathouse was killed
jumped through the window, breaking
the sash and was killed by his own
party, they thinking it was me trying to
make my escape. The party then
withdrew.

They returned the next day and
burned down an old man named
Spencer's house and Greathouse's
house also.

Finally, Billy described his problems with
Pat Garrett and John Chisum.

Sheriff Garrett acting under Chisum's
orders went to the Portales and found
nothing. On the way back he went to
Mr. Yerby's ranch and took a pair of
mules of mine, which I had left with Mr.
Bowdre who is in charge of Mr. Yerby's
cattle. He (Garrett) claimed they were
stolen and even if they were not he had

the right to confiscate any outlaws property. I have been at Sumner since I left Lincoln making my living gambling. The mules were bought by me. The truth is known by the best citizens around Sumner. J.S. Chisum got me into this trouble and was benefitted thousands by it and is now doing all he can against me.

Yours respectfully,
William Bonney

"You think it will do any good," I asked.

"Ira Leonard is still trying to help out with my pardon. I figured the fight at the Greathouse ranch might be another bump in the road," Billy stared across the counter, waiting for my endorsement.

"I suppose the letter can't hurt. At this point, do you really think Wallace will come through with his end of the bargain?"

"It's about all I can hope for," Billy admitted. For the first time since I had met him when he was seventeen, his confidence seemed to waver.

"Even if the pardon was still good, you would have to submit to arrest and take your chances with Judge Bristol."

Billy looked at me and shook his head.

"I think with Garrett in office, they'll be coming at you from every direction."

"My informants tell me that very thing," Billy admitted. "There's an outfit in White Oaks led by Charlie Siringo coming this way. Frank Stewart is leading another band of Texans down from Anton Chico. Garrett has gone back to Roswell for reinforcements."

"Might be a good time to leave here, Billy."

"I intend to," Billy tipped back his hat as if he were stalling for time. "There's no other selection. Tom and I have decided to visit his grandmother in Texas. We should make it by Christmas."

"I don't think I'd wait that long." I hesitated for a moment and decided to tell him about Danny. "My brother, Danny, was killed in the ring a few weeks back. He hit his head on the corner post. They carried him out dead."

Billy's looked discouraged, "I'll be damned."

"It was a sad day for our family. That's why all your friends want you to clear out before something happens to you."

"They won't catch me, Robert. They're a day late and a dollar short. Anyway, I don't mind going out in a fight. I always figured it could end that way. I won't let them make a spectacle of me. To be led around in chains and swing

229

from a rope."

"There may not be much time, Billy."

"You've been a good friend, Robert. Since I showed up here that fall. Tom and I will leave inside a week."

"Okay, Billy," I reached across the counter to shake hands.

"Adios," Billy pulled down his hat and left to get his horse.

25

For a week after Billy had posted his letter to Governor Wallace, I heard nothing about Billy or his friends. I thought that Billy and Tom O'Folliard had gone to Texas as planned. I knew that Charlie Siringo, Frank Stewart and Pat Garrett were on their way with a pile of deputies.

Any hope of a clean start for Billy and Tom ended on December 19th. Billy and his gang had been given false information by Manuel Brazil that Garrett and his men had returned to Roswell. Instead, they were waiting in ambush at Fort Sumner.

Billy Bonney, Tom O'Folliard, Charley Bowdre, Dave Rudabaugh, Tom Pickett and Billy Wilson made a fatal decision to ride into Sumner that night. Garrett had guessed that their first stop would be the Indian hospital where Charlie's wife lived. Garrett had his men waiting in the shadows outside the building as the riders slowly approached.

As the group horsemen reached the porch, with O'Folliard in the lead, Garrett yelled to them to throw up their hands. The six men wheeled on their horses to escape. Tom O'Folliard was shot through the chest.

Garrett had no warrant for O'Folliard. Jim East helped the unlucky twenty-two year old off his horse. They carried him inside the building. East tended to the dying man while Garrett and the others resumed their game of cards. In less than an hour, Tom O'Folliard was dead.

Billy and the others disappeared in the darkness and rode to the Wilcox-Brazil ranch to regroup. They spent the next day glassing the area from a hill above the ranch. They expected Garrett and Stewart to track them to the ranch, despite the heavy snowfall.

On the night of December 22nd, Billy and his gang made the decision to head east across the Texas border. They took some provisions and made camp in an abandoned rock house about ten miles east of the Wilcox-Brazil ranch.

At about the time that Billy's gang had left for Texas, Garrett and his posse of eighteen men had left Fort Sumner. When the posse reached the Wilcox-Brazil ranch, they discovered that the outlaws had ridden east. Instead of spending the night at the ranch, Garrett ordered his men to take up the trail of the outlaws, which was easy to follow in the fresh snow.

Just before dawn, Garrett and his men discovered several horses tied outside the rock house at Stinking Spring. There was one open door and no windows in the twenty-foot long structure. Garrett had his men fanned out around the opening. Garrett told them that if a man walked through the door wearing a Mexican sombrero, they were to shoot to kill.

At first light, a man wearing a sombrero walked out of the door with a feedbag. The posse opened fire. Charlie Bowdre was hit several times including a shot to the chest. He stumbled back into the rock house. Billy Wilson yelled to the posse that they had hit Charlie and he was coming out.

As Charlie Bowdre staggered toward his killers, it was clear that he was mortally wounded. As he approached Garrett, he muttered, "I wish." Then, he fell dead in the snow. In his pursuit of Billy, Garrett had now killed his two closest friends.

It was clear to Garrett that Billy had brought

his bay mare into the house for a mounted escape. When the gang tried to bring another horse into the house, Garrett shot the animal in the doorway. With the dead horse blocking the door, the four men inside had no escape route.

The standoff went on throughout the day. Occasional shots were fired. Garrett ordered the men inside the rock house to surrender. Billy told Garrett that he could go to hell. It was clear that Billy wanted to hold out until dark. He would try to make his escape before the moon came up.

Late in the afternoon, against Billy's wishes, Dave Rudabaugh attached a white cloth to the end of his rifle and waved it out the doorway. Garrett ordered him to come out with his hands up and he would not be shot. Rudabaugh walked out and conferred with Garrett. He was told to assure the other three men that they would be protected if they would surrender.

Rudabaugh returned to the rock house with the message from Garrett. Wilson and Pickett wanted to surrender. Billy argued that it would be dark in a few hours and they would have a chance to escape. Billy strongly argued his case, but he was out numbered. In the late afternoon, the four men came out with their hands up.

When Billy saw the scattering of deputies, he told Garrett that he thought the house was surrounded by a hundred Texans or he would have never come out. Barney Mason, Billy's old friend from Fort Sumner, raised his rifle to shoot the young outlaw. Jim East pointed his revolver at Mason. East swore that if Mason shot Billy, he would kill Mason.

The four men were allowed to eat. They were then taken back to the Wilcox-Brazil ranch, along with the body of Charlie Bowdre. The posse and the prisoners spent the night at the ranch. The next morning, the four men were taken to Fort Sumner to be fitted with leg irons.

When the posse and the prisoners reached Manuela Bowdre's house on Christmas Eve, she rushed out the door to meet her husband. When she saw one of the posse men riding his horse, she began to cry and swear at Garrett. When Jim East and Louis Bousman carried Charlie's corpse into the house, Manuela attacked East with a branding iron.

From a distance, Pat Garrett promised Manuela Bowdre that he would pay for a new suit of clothes and Charlie's burial. Like so many times in Garrett's life, this was a hollow promise to pay. Anyway, it was the least he could do for mistakenly killing her husband.

As the four men were being fitted for chains at the blacksmith's shop, Delvina Maxwell approached Garrett. She told Garrett that Dona Luz Maxwell, who was the mother of Pete and Paulita, would like her daughter to have an opportunity to say goodbye to Billy. Garrett agreed. He sent Jim East and Lee Hall to escort Billy to the Maxwell house.

When the group arrived, Dona Luz asked if Billy and Paulita could say their goodbyes in a private room. The deputies declined. The two sweethearts were allowed to embrace in an extended goodbye kiss before Billy was taken away and loaded into a wagon.

Progress was slow as the deputies and the wagon headed north up the Pecos over the new snow. They reached the Gerhardt Ranch late that night where they were fed. At first light, they continued up the road to Puerto de Luna.

When they reached Padre Polaco's cantina on the afternoon of Christmas, they were treated to a fine meal. Like all the ranchers in the area, Alexander Grzelachowski was pleased to know that the band of rustlers had been captured. He pulled out all the stops to see that Garrett and his prisoners were well fed.

After supper, the slow moving caravan continued north toward Las Vegas. They traveled through the night and reached the old town plaza the next morning. A huge crowd had gathered. Some of the citizens wanted to get their hands on Dave Rudabaugh who had killed Deputy Lino Valdez earlier that year. The rest had turned out to see the young outlaw who had been made famous by the territorial newspapers.

Billy seemed to enjoy himself as he looked over the crowd. When he saw an acquaintance, he called out, "I just stopped by to see if you fellas were behaving yourselves." While the other three prisoners looked downcast, Billy was in a friendly mood. After the four men were locked up in jail, Garrett and his men spent the afternoon accepting free drinks in the saloons around the plaza.

The next day, while the four prisoners were changing into a clean set of clothes, two local reporters were allowed into the jail to interview them. The Gazette man filed the following story:

> *Billy the Kid and Billy Wilson, who were shackled together, stood patiently while a blacksmith took off their shackles and bracelets to allow them an opportunity to make a change of clothing. Both prisoners watched the operation which was to set them free for*

a short while, but Wilson scarcely raised his eyes and spoke but once or twice to his compadre. Bonney, on the other hand, was light and chipper and very communicative, laughing, joking and chatting with the bystanders.

"You appear to take it easy," I suggested.

"Yes. What's the use in looking on the gloomy side of everything? The laugh's on me this time," he said. Then, looking around the placita, he asked, "Is the jail at Santa Fe any better than this? This is a terrible place to put a fellow." He asked the same question to everyone who came near him and when he learned that there was nothing better in store for him, he shrugged his shoulders and said something about putting up with what he had to.

He was the attraction of the show, and as he stood there, lightly kicking the toes of his boots on the stone pavement to keep his feet warm, one would scarcely mistrust that he was the hero of the "Forty Thieves" romance that this paper has been running in serial form for six weeks or more.

There was nothing very mannish

238

about him in appearance, for he looked and acted a mere boy. He is about five feet eight or nine inches tall, slightly built and lithe, weighing about 140; a frank open countenance, looking like a school boy, with the traditional silky fuzz on his upper lip; clear blue eyes with a roguish snap about them; light hair and complexion. He is, in all, quite a handsome looking fellow, the only imperfection being two prominent front teeth, slightly protruding like squirrel's teeth, and he has agreeable and winning ways.

After the change of clothes, three of the prisoners were re-shackled and loaded into a wagon to be taken to the train station. Garrett had no federal warrant for Pickett so he was left in the Las Vegas jail. When the deputies and the prisoners arrived at the train siding, there was an angry group of Hispanos waiting. They were determined to hang Dave Rudabaugh. Garrett explained to Sheriff Romero, that his federal warrant trumped the local charges. Romero disagreed. The crowd failed to disburse.

All the while, Billy leaned out a window and carried on a conversation with onlookers. He invited them to visit him in Santa Fe. When Garrett told the prisoners that he would arm them if the mob attacked the train, Billy told him to give him his Winchester and he would lick the whole crowd. Billy then told Garrett, in a disappointed tone, that the men in the mob would not fight.

The train finally left the station on the short journey to Santa Fe. While in route, Billy became friends with Miguel Otero, who was from a prominent land grant family. His father ran the bank in Las Vegas. Otero was about the same age as Billy. He was so fascinated with the personality of the young outlaw that he decided to stay in Santa Fe for several days. Otero engaged in long conversations with Billy and brought bakery goods and chewing gum to him. Miguel Otero later became the first Hispano governor of New Mexico Territory.

26

Susan and I read all of the newspaper accounts of Billy's capture and his lock up in Santa Fe. The folks around Sumner were angry about the killings of Tom O'Folliard and Charlie Bowdre. The two men had been working at the Thomas Yerby ranch. Both were well liked. Bowdre was married. The common sentiment was that Garrett had overstepped his authority when he had waited in ambush and killed them.

The politicians in Santa Fe and the large cattle outfits could not have been happier. The constant reminder of their theft of Mexican land was locked away in the Santa Fe jail. It was a near certainty that he would be hanged.

I had nothing but time to ponder these events. It seemed to me that Garrett was in a hurry to establish a reputation for himself. He had grown up in a prominent family in Louisiana. His father had owned a plantation and forty slaves. When the war ruined them financially, Garrett had gone to Texas to establish himself. He had tried his luck at farming and buffalo killing. He had arrived penniless at Fort Sumner.

After he had arrived here, he had gotten work with Pete Maxwell. Shortly thereafter, they had had a falling out. One rumor indicated that the issue was an unpaid loan. Another rumor had it that Garrett had carved up Maxwell's cattle in his butcher shop.

Garrett had worked as a bartender at Beaver Smith's saloon. In fact, he and Billy had run a Monte game there. The two would often gamble together. They would even stake one another. It seemed to me that Garrett resented the adulation that Billy received everywhere he went. Garrett could simply not match his humor or his ability to make friends. Garrett may have felt that Billy was poorly bred and undeserving of all the admiration.

When Dona Luz Maxwell made a request of Garrett to allow Paulita and Billy to say their goodbyes before Billy was hauled off the jail, I thought that there might be some meaning to that. It was known around Sumner that the two were sweethearts, but it seemed odd that the mother would ask for time for her daughter to say goodbye to a young outlaw. There was a rumor that Paulita was with child. That may have explained her mother's request.

Billy had told the Gazette reporter that he didn't want to look on the gloomy side, but his future was certainly gloomy. It had been clear to me for some time that Governor Wallace would not be able to honor his promise to pardon Billy even though Billy had kept his part of the agreement and had testified before two grand juries.

The difficulty for Wallace was the killing of Joe Grant and the death of Jimmy Carlyle, which the newspapers were quick to blame on Billy. There had also been a lot of cattle stolen since the two had made their bargain. The dignitaries in Santa Fe and the big ranchers east of the Pecos would be outraged if Billy were set free.

A week after Billy had been delivered to Santa Fe, Pat Garrett came into the post office on his return to Roswell. He had two letters to post. One was to Louisiana and another to Santa Fe. Like most folks around Fort Sumner, I was angry with Garrett over the deaths of Charlie Bowdre and Tom O'Folliard. I bore no grudge for his arrest of Billy.

"Did you collect your reward," I asked.

Garrett ignored the question and placed the two letters on the counter.

"It doesn't look good for Billy, does it," I asked.

Garrett stared at me for a moment, "It looks like your little friend will hang for his trouble."

The dismissive comment angered me, "I suppose that would suit you fine, Pat."

"I was just doing my sworn duty," Garrett sounded bored with the conversation.

"Well, you're off to a fine start."

"One item scratched off the list is all," Garrett had the superior tone of a man with new found importance.

"It might've been better for Billy if you had executed him like the other two." My temper had kicked in. All I could think of was working that exposed rib cage with both hands.

Garrett looked at my waist to see that I wasn't wearing a gun. "I have better things to do than lip off with some postal clerk," he said calmly. "See that those letters gets out." With that last bit of superiority, he turned and left.

When New Years Day, 1881, arrived, there was little reason to celebrate around Fort Sumner. The young man who had brought good humor and respect for Mexican people was rotting away in a jail cell in Santa Fe. The New

Year's dance at Sumner was so lifeless that they postponed any further dances. It seemed that there could be no baile without Billy.

Paulita Maxwell would come to Sunnyside every few weeks to post a letter to Billy. Within a week, Billy would send a reply. Paulita had become a dejected little person. There was nothing I could say that would cheer her up. All she read and heard was that Billy would certainly be hanged. To a girl of sixteen, that image must have been unimaginable.

I felt obligated to send a letter to Billy, but I never did. I knew of no way to encourage him. Cheer is in short supply while the hangman waits. Other than Paulita, he must have felt that he had been abandoned by all of his friends.

When I read that his trial would be held in Mesilla, I knew there was no hope for an acquittal. Billy's enemies from the Lincoln County War, including Jimmy Dolan, Jesse Evans and John Kinney, were from Mesilla. More ominous would be the presiding judge. Warren Bristol was an avowed enemy of John Tunstall and the Regulators. The only question was when Billy would be hanged.

At the end of March 1881, Billy was taken by train to La Mesilla. The first charge he faced was for the death of Buckshot Roberts. Billy's attorney, Ira Leonard, was able to get this charge dismissed due to a question of jurisdiction. The gunfight between Roberts and the Regulators had taken place at Blazer's Mill, which was on the Mescalero Apache Reservation. This made the crime a federal matter.

Judge Bristol agreed that Dona Anna County did not have jurisdiction in the Buckshot Roberts case. Bristol dismissed the case in order to proceed with the charge of the murder of Sheriff William Brady. Before the trial began, Judge Bristol ordered Ira Leonard to step down as Billy's attorney.

This unexpected move was a setback to Billy's defense. Ira Leonard had been in regular contact with Billy since the end of the Lincoln County War. He had been actively corresponding with Governor Wallace in an attempt to win the pardon that Billy had been promised. Instead, Billy would be represented by Albert J. Fountain, who was not familiar with Billy or the details of the five-month war in Lincoln.

Simon Newcomb, who was a close friend of former D.A. William Rynerson, would act as prosecutor. Rynerson had bankrolled Jimmy Dolan. He had allowed Jesse Evans and John Kinney to dodge a number of murder charges in

Dona Ana County. It appeared that the deck was stacked.

Set to testify for the prosecution were Jimmy Dolan, George Peppin and Billy Matthews. These were three of Billy's greatest enemies during The Lincoln county War. Billy was one of seven Regulators who fired at Sheriff Brady. His accomplices were dead or gone. When all the testimony has been heard, Judge Bristol ordered the jury to bring in a guilty verdict.

On April 9th, after a short deliberation, the jury delivered a verdict of guilty. Four days later, Billy was brought back to appear before Judge Bristol for sentencing. Bristol ordered that Billy to be taken back to Lincoln where he would be hanged on Friday, May 13th. When Billy was given a chance to speak, he said nothing.

Three days later, Billy was put in a wagon under heavy guard and taken to Lincoln. Included in the seven guards were two of Billy's worst enemies. Bob Olinger had shot John Jones four times in the back. The Jones family had nursed Billy back to health after he had nearly died on his way to Seven Rivers. John Jones was Billy's closest friend at that time. After John's murder, Billy had ridden to Seven Rivers to promise Heiskell and Maam Jones that he would take care of Bob Olinger.

Also included in the group of guards was John Kinney. The renowned cattle thief from Mesilla had burned down the town of San Patricio under orders from Sheriff Peppin. Many of Billy's friends in the placita had lost their homes and their livestock. Billy had wounded Kinney in the face during his escape from Alexander McSween's burning house in Lincoln. In terms of murder and stolen livestock, John Kinney had no equal in the territory with the possible exception of Jesse Evans.

Lincoln County had bought the building, formerly known as the House, when Murphy and Dolan had gone bankrupt. The two-story structure now served as a courthouse and jail. Billy was assigned a room on the second floor in the northeast corner. He was chained to the floor and under constant guard.

Two deputies alternately guarded Billy. James Bell played cards with Billy and brought him chewing gum. Bob Olinger poked and taunted Billy at every opportunity. Billy remained calm in the face of his tormentor while he bided his time. With three weeks left before he was to be hanged, Billy concentrated on what might be one last chance to escape.

27

On April 28th, two weeks before he was to be hanged, word reached Fort Sumner that Billy had broken out of jail in Lincoln. Details were at a minimum. A traveler from Lincoln reported that Billy had killed two deputies and made his escape while Pat Garrett was in White Oaks collecting taxes. In the New Mexico Territory, a sheriff received a percentage of all revenue that he collected. It seemed that Garrett's never ending quest for money had resulted in the escape of his notorious young prisoner.

It was thought that Billy was on his way to Mexico where he could avoid capture. I went into Sumner that evening to have a beer and catch up on any new information. When I walked into Bab Hargrove's saloon, the first person I encountered was Barney Mason.

Mason stood against the bar while he sipped his beer. He looked unnerved and for good reason. He had been with the posse that had surrounded Billy at the rock house at Stinking Spring. Garrett had executed Charley Bowdre with no warning. When Billy surrendered, Mason wanted to kill him. He was stopped by Jim East. Now, Billy was loose and Barney was nervous.

I ordered a beer and stood next to Mason, "What's the story, Barney?"

"The Kid's broke out of jail in Lincoln." There was worry in his voice. "He's killed Bell and Olinger. I hear Pat was in White Oaks."

"There was bad blood between Billy and Olinger," I reminded Barney. "After Olinger shot John Jones in the back."

"Nobody knows where's he's heading," Mason explained. "Likely he'll cross into Mexico, but it wouldn't surprise me to see him ride into Sumner."

"He might have unfinished business here." Mason had no way of knowing that I knew of the incident at Stinking Spring.

Barney looked up at me, "The Kid's loose again."

"He'd be wise to head for Mexico, but you never know."

Mason finished his beer and left. Some Hispano drovers had wandered in and were speaking excitedly in Spanish. I heard "Beely" or "Beelito" or "Chivato" as they celebrated his freedom. I figured most of the folks around Sumner would be happy with the news of Billy's escape. Barney Mason was not one of them.

Susan was relieved that Billy had avoided the hangman. She prayed that he had gone to Mexico. The killing of two deputies during his escape would make it impossible for him to remain in the territory. I wasn't certain that he would run to Mexico. Billy had an uncommon lack of fear. Our young friend tempted fate at every turn.

Sure enough, a week after his escape, Billy walked into the post office.

"My God, Billy."

"How are you, Robert," he reached over the counter to shake my hand.

"To be honest, I never expected to see you again."

"My mother once told me that if I ever had trouble with the law, I may not live to see twenty one. She didn't miss by much." He was the same friendly kid. He could find humor in the most miserable circumstance. The big smile was there, but the happy eyes were gone.

"How in hell did you get out of there?"

Billy motioned for me to come around to the back of the building where he had tied his horse. He wanted to be able to watch the road. He put his right foot on the bottom rail of the fence and leaned back against the top rail. I never knew Billy to look agitated or uncomfortable. It was as if he were going to tell me how many fish he had caught.

"I had begun to think I might never find a way out of there. I figured maybe my run of luck had ended. Gauss smuggled me in some strychnine, which I held in my boot. I wasn't going to let my friends in Lincoln see me dangle from that rope.

"I was told a gun would be left in the privy, but a week went by and it never appeared. I kept waiting for the proper moment for a fallback plan, but Olinger was always on top of me with that shotgun and Garrett was in the next room.

"When I heard that Garrett was going to White Oaks to collect taxes, I figured that would be my only chance. Once Garrett got back, it would be a much tougher road. That afternoon, when Olinger took the other prisoners across the street to Wortley's for supper, it left just me and Bell.

"I told Bell that I needed to use the privy so he unbolted me from the floor and we headed out back. Still no pistol was stashed there. As we came up the stairs, I moved slowly as if my leg irons were a burden. Bell was just a step below me. When I reached the top step, I swung around and hit Bell along side the head with my bracelets. It was a heavy blow and knocked him to his knees.

"I dived down and went for his pistol. As I tried to pull it free, he grabbed the barrel. In the struggle, the gun went off, hitting him in the side, under the arm. He let out a groan and stumbled down the stairs.

"I rushed into Garrett's office and grabbed Bob Olinger's shotgun. He had poked me with that Whitney every day since we left Mesilla. I knew the son-of-a-bitch would be coming and I figured he would have to go through the gate just under the window where they had kept me locked down to the floor.

"Sure enough, here comes Bob. I stood to the side of the window until he stepped through the gate. I leaned out the window and leveled the shotgun. I said, "Hello, old boy," When he looked up, I let him have it with both loads of buckshot. That made good on a promise I made to the Jones family after Olinger shot John in the back.

"I was on my way out, but there was still work to do. I went out onto the porch and hollered for Gauss throw up something to try and bust loose my leg irons. He found a miner's pick and tossed it up on the porch. I told him to saddle a horse and bring it around. I was nervous as a cat as I worked on those chains. I finally broke one leg free.

"A crowd had come out onto the street and I told them to get back inside. I told them I didn't want to hurt anyone, but I was fighting for my life up there. Gauss finally brought Billy Burt's little black horse around so I went downstairs. It was time to clear out of there.

"When I tried to mount Burt's horse, he was spooked by the leg chain and threw me off. A prisoner by the name of Nunnelly caught the horse and brought him around to me. He was a fella from Tularosa. I told him to tell Garrett that I made him do it.

"I finally calmed the animal down and got into the saddle. I waved adios to the folks who had come out to see me off. I told them not to look for me this side of Ireland. I gave the horse a kick and we trotted out of town heading west. I felt so free I started singing."

"Brennan on the Moor?"

"No," Billy shook his head. "A little ballad. I heard Mother sing it a hundred times."

I go to the plains with much sadness,
And never again shall return.
And with patience I'll wait for my passing.
And no one will weep when I'm gone.

For a few moments, Billy stared at the trees along the river. I felt sure that he was thinking about his mother. Perhaps, he wondered what she would have thought of the strange direction that his life had taken since he left Silver City. He was fifteen at the time. He had wandered for six years. I knew that the most difficult part of his journey lay ahead.

"At he edge of town, I stopped and bought a rope from a friend named Ortiz. Once I was clear of town, I crossed the Bonito and headed into the hills toward Agua Azul. I staked down the horse and spent the night there. Gauss had tied two of his red blankets to the back of the saddle.

"The next night I made it to Las Tablas. I went in after dark. I stayed with a friend, which I shall leave unnamed. He helped get me shed of the leg irons and fed me for three days. At night, I would sleep in the trees above his place.

Burt's horse broke free of his tether that first night at Las Tablas. He was on his way back to Lincoln. Billy Burt loved that little black horse. I intended to have him returned.

"My friend loaned me a new mount. I ducked and dodged for a few days, visiting some friends that wouldn't betray me. I thought of going to Old Mexico, but I figured the longer I stayed down there, the poorer I'd be.

"I worked my way back toward Sumner. On the second morning heading in this direction, my horse was spooked and ran off. I walked about twenty miles until I got to a sheep camp at Buffalo Arroyo.

"Late that afternoon, who should ride into camp but Barney Mason and a fella named Cureton. When Mason saw me, he turned and left out of there, presto chango. That little weasel wanted to kill me when we surrendered to Garrett at Stinking Spring. If Jim East hadn't leveled his pistol on Mason that afternoon, I'd be laying there alongside Charley and Tom in the cemetery.

"Two days later I'm over at Taiban and who comes through with his family loaded up in a wagon headed south toward Roswell? It was ol' Barney himself. He had the look you did when I came through that door a few minutes ago. His eyes were this big," Billy made two circles with his thumb and middle finger. "I may catch up with Barney down the road, but I couldn't settle him in front of the wife and kids."

"You've busted open a hornet's nest this time," I stared at Billy.

"Olinger got what was coming to him. I wish I hadn't shot Bell. He treated me real decent while he was on guard. We played cards and swapped lies. He even brought me chewing gum. If I could have got his gun, I would have locked him up and waited for Olinger. Bell's the only man I ever killed that didn't have it coming to him."

"Paulita will be happy to see you. She's been a sad girl the past few months."

"I stopped to see her last night. She cried and ran up when she spotted me. That girl is the only one to write to me while I was counting the days in jail. I can't ever forget that."

"What about Pete?"

Billy looked at the ground and thought for a moment, "Pete and me have always been on good terms. I'm guessing that he might rather not have me around Sumner. Harboring a criminal isn't recommended for a man in his position."

"What about Paulita?"

"I asked her to consider leaving with me. She said she would think on it. I told her if I could get as far as California, I might send for her. She found that notion more agreeable."

"So now what?"

"I've had two weeks to consider this thing," Billy pushed away from the fence and reached for the reins of his horse. "I wouldn't know anybody in Mexico or California. Besides, I've got no money to get there. I have friends in every sheep camp for miles around. For now, I'll lay low and watch my back."

"I've got a hundred and twenty dollars in a flour sack behind the drawer in there," I said. "I don't know how far it will get you, but you're welcome to it."

Billy looked at me for a few moments. "No," he said. "I doubt I could ever pay it back."

"Write us a letter from California. We'll call it square."

"No. You and Susan may need that money down the road. Thanks, just the same."

As was his custom, Billy reached out to shake hands. He was always a back slapper and a hand shaker. And a smiler. There was no smile this time as he looked me in the eye and nodded. He mounted his horse and looked down at me. He tipped his black sombrero and rode off.

That was the last time I ever saw Billy. I would hear that he had been in Fort Sumner at night, but he would leave before dawn the next day. The word was he was at Arenoso or Canaditas. He would sometimes stay at Frank Lobato's sheep camp. The carefree hero of the Lincoln County War had been reduced to living in the shadows.

28

On the morning of July 15th, we got the news that Billy Bonney had been killed at Fort Sumner. He had walked into Pete Maxwell's bedroom around midnight and been shot by Pat Garrett. That's all we knew. They planned to lay Billy to rest that afternoon.

Susan did not cry as she had when Danny died. She had a hollow, distant look. Nothing was said as we put on our Sunday best. I put the mule in harness and brought the buggy around to the house. I helped Susan up into her seat. Lonesome Joe jumped in and took his position in front of us. I shook the reins and we started south on the river road.

Storm clouds had gathered to the south. You could smell rain in the air. It was a fitting day for a burial.

"He never had a chance," Susan said quietly. "From the time his mother died, he had to fend for himself any way he could. He was a good-hearted boy in the company of thieves and killers. With all that, he and his friend from Oklahoma wanted to start their own ranch."

"It looked encouraging for a short time with Tunstall."

Susan looked over at me, "Is there any doubt that he would have prospered if John Tunstall hadn't been killed? Or he had gotten a place of his own. That boy was so clever. He had a way with people like no one I've ever known. I'll tell you one thing. He was more outstanding than Pat Garrett will ever be."

I now realized that Susan's distant look was more from anger than sorrow.

"Will anyone remember the way he treated the Mexican people," she went on. "The way he made them feel, proud. He made such an effort to respect them. He learned their language. He adopted their customs. He really was one of them. Now, what? The cattlemen are happy. The politicians in Santa Fe will congratulate each other while they drink their imported brandy. He amounted to more than the whole lot of them."

We rode along in silence for a ways. I knew

that Susan was fond of Billy, but her anger caught me off guard.

"At least he wasn't hanged," I suggested. "It was the only thing he really was afraid of. Not dying, but the shame of it."

"Pat Garrett," Susan wasn't finished. "He'll be toasted by all the dignitaries in the capitol. The man who made the territory safe for all the swindlers in Santa Fe. And, the big cattle outfits. Billy was a reminder, you know. Of the treachery that was employed to steal the land from the native people. Who stands up for the Mexican people? Certainly not Pat Garrett."

"I think it was the girls," I had been thinking about this since Billy returned to Fort Sumner. "He was seeing Nasaria Yerby out at their ranch. He spent a lot of time up there. He was friendly with Abrana Garcia. I noticed them walking in the peach orchard out behind Bob Hargrove's place one evening.

"You know he was sweet on Paulita Maxwell. She was the only girl who wrote to him while he was in jail. Maybe she was the girl that Billy couldn't have. The jewel of Fort Sumner. And there was Celsa Gutierrez. She made no secret of her love for Billy even though she was married. And Garrett's sister-in-law."

"It was more than the girls," Susan stared

ahead at the road. She spoke with a weary voice, "This was the only place he had ever been respected or admired. To the Mexican people, he was like a saint. He was always proud to honor them. I fear it will be a long while before they forget his passing."

When we arrived at Sumner, we went directly to the cemetary, east of the fort. Vincente Otero and Jesus Silva had finished digging a grave. Billy was to be buried next to Charlie Bowdre and Tom O'Folliard. Pat Garrett had ended each of their troubles. Ambush was his chosen method. Now, these three young men would rest side by side.

From our right, a horse drawn wagon moved toward us. It looked like everyone in town was following that wagon. As the makeshift hearse drew closer, I could see the short, wide frame of Delvina Maxwell. She was alone, out in front. As the procession grew nearer, I could see she was weeping and blowing her nose into a handkerchief.

At the rear were Pat Garrett and Pete Maxwell along with deputies John Poe and Kip McKinney. Garrett and the two deputies wore their side arms. Paulita and Dona Luz Maxwell walked in front of them.

When the wagon reached the gravesite, four

Mexican men lifted the simple wooden box out of the back. They carefully lowered the box into the grave with two ropes. There was no priest or minister at Fort Sumner. A man named Pruitt read a verse from Psalms, "He maketh me to lie down in green pastures. He leadeth me beside the still waters...."

Many of the Mexican women were crying. An occasional wail would come up from the crowd. The men looked downcast. There was little emotion in their faces as they slowly marched forward. I thought that Pat Garrett and Pete Maxwell looked uncomfortable. On edge.

The ropes were withdrawn from under the coffin. Otero and Silva began to shovel dirt into the hole. When the mound was completed and tamped down, the Mexican women began to place flowers on the grave. Paulita Maxwell placed a bouquet of wild flowers beneath the simple cross. By the time the women were finished, all three graves were covered in flowers.

There was nothing more to be done. No family to console. No priest. No bagpipes. Only a new grave and a gathering of sad people. Susan and I got into the buggy and started north on the road to Sunnyside.

"It's such a shame," Susan finally said.

"Those were three good boys. So well mannered and intelligent."

"It was their bad luck that Garrett was elected," I said.

"Bad fortune does not make any of this right," Susan said. "All three were killed by a man who was in hiding. They had no chance. Where's the justice in that?"

I was not as quick to defend Billy as Susan was. I thought he had made a deadly mistake when he partnered up with Dave Rudabaugh, Billy Wilson and Tom Pickett. These were wanted men with few redeeming features.

Rudabaugh had come from Dodge City with a reputation as a cold killer. Wilson had been shoving the queer in White Oaks and Lincoln. This brought federal agents to New Mexico to investigate the counterfeiting scheme. Pickett had been a Texas Ranger, but he was now wanted for stagecoach robbery. Billy had drifted into a life of cattle rustling with known criminals.

After the Lincoln County War, Billy's three years around Fort Sumner were nothing short of a moving fiesta. From Anton Chico to Puerto de Luna to Fort Sumner, Billy never missed a dance or wedding celebration. He gambled and raced horses. To his many friends, he may have been the Prince of the Pecos, but he was a wanted man. In the end, he had no plan other than day to day. He had to know the law was near.

It was through Deputy John Poe that we learned the details of Billy's death that night. Pat Garrett was tight lipped about the matter. As printed in the Santa Fe New Mexican, here is Poe's account of the night of July 14, 1881:

> *I proposed that, before leaving, we should go to the residence of Peter Maxwell, a man I had never seen but who, by reason of being a leading citizen and having large property interests, should, according to my reasoning, be glad to furnish such information as he might have to aid us in ridding the country of a man who was looked on as a scourge and curse to all law-abiding people. Garrett agreed to this and led us from the orchard by circuitous bypaths to the Maxwell residence, a building used as officer's quarters during the days when a garrison of troops had been maintained at the fort. The house was very long, one story adobe, flush to the street, with a porch*

on the south side-the direction from which we approached. The premises were all enclosed by a paling fence, one side of which ran parallel and along the edge of the street up to and across the edge of the porch to the corner of the building. When we arrived at the house, Garrett said to me, "This is Maxwell's room in the corner. You fellows wait here while I go in and talk to him." He stepped onto the porch and entered Maxwell's room through an open door (left open on account of the extremely warm weather), while McKinney and I stopped outside. McKinney squatted on the outside of the fence, and I sat on the edge of the porch in the small open gateway leading from the street to the porch.

It should be mentioned here that up to this moment I had never seen Billy the Kid nor Maxwell, which fact, in view of the events transpiring immediately afterward, placed me at an extreme disadvantage. Probably not more than thirty seconds after Garrett had entered Maxwell's room, my attention was attracted, from where I sat in the little gateway, to a man approaching me on the inside of the fence, some forty or fifty steps away. I observed that he was only partially dressed and was both bareheaded and barefooted (or, rather, had only socks on his feet) and it seemed to me that he was fastening his trousers as he came toward me at a very brisk walk. As Maxwell's was the one place in Fort Sumner that I considered above suspicion; I was extremely off my guard. I thought the man approaching was either Maxwell of some guest of his. He came on until he was almost within arms-length of where I sat before he saw me, as I was partially concealed from his view by the post of the gate.

Upon seeing me, he covered me with his six-shooter as quick as lightning, sprang onto the porch, calling out in Spanish, "Quien es?" At the same time he backed away from me toward the door which Garrett only a few seconds before had passed, repeating his query, "Who is it?" in Spanish several times. As I stood up and advanced toward him, telling not to be alarmed, that he should not be hurt, still without the least suspicion that this was the very man we were looking for. As I moved toward him trying to reassure him, he backed into the doorway of Maxwell's room, where he hesitated for a moment, his body concealed by the thick adobe wall at the side of the doorway. He put out his head and asked in Spanish for the forth or fifth time who I was. I was within a few feet of him when he disappeared into the room.

After this, and until after the shooting, I was unable to see what took place on account of the darkness in the room, but plainly heard what was said. An instant after the man had left the door, I heard a voice inquire in a sharp tone, "Pete, who are those men on the outside?" An instant later a shot was fired in the room, followed immediately by what everyone within hearing distance thought were two other shots. However, there were only two shots fired, the third report, as we learned afterward, being caused by the rebound of the second bullet, which had struck the adobe wall and rebounded against the headboard of the wooden bedstead. I heard a groan and one or two gasps from where I stood in the doorway, as if someone were dying in the room. An instant later, Garrett came out, brushing against me as he passed. He stood by me close to the wall at the side of the door and said to me, "That's the Kid that came in there onto me, and I think I have got him." I said, "Pat, the Kid would not come to this place; you shot the wrong man.

Upon my saying this, Garrett seemed to be in doubt himself, but he quickly spoke up and said, "I am sure that was him, for I know his voice too well to be mistaken." The remark of Garrett's relieved me of considerable apprehension, as I had felt almost certain that someone else had been killed. A moment after Garrett came out of the door, Pete Maxwell rushed squarely onto me in a frantic effort to get out of the room, and I certainly would have shot him but for Garrett's striking my gun down, saying, "Don't shoot Maxwell." By this time I had begun to realize that we were in a place which was not above suspicion and as Garrett was so positive that the Kid was inside, I came to the conclusion that we were up against a case of "kill or be killed", such as we had heard from the beginning

*realized would be the case whenever we
came upon the Kid.*

*A candle was lit and placed outside
the window. In the dim flicker of light,
a body could be seen lying motionless on
the floor. Garrett's first shot had hit
Billy in the chest, just above the heart.
His second shot had missed and hit the
far wall and rebounded into the wooden
headboard. Billy had not fired a shot.*

I considered Poe's words. Why hadn't Billy
simply backed away from the two strangers
while he had them covered with his revolver?
He would have instantly known that these two
men were a danger to him. Why would he go
past them and into a dark room where he would
be cornered? If they had attempted to draw
their weapons as he backed away, Billy could
easily have shot them at such a close distance. It
made no sense to me.

If Billy had backed up along the picket fence,
he could have ducked around the corner and fled
into the night. The two men would not have
dared to follow him in the dark. Someone
would have brought a horse around and Billy
could have ridden off to safety. I thought there
must be something missing from Poe's carefully

crafted account.

Death had come quickly to our young friend. I knew that it could have been worse. Billy's greatest fear was to be arrested and hanged. He had promised me that he would not allow himself to become a spectacle. While he had awaited the hangman in Lincoln, he kept a vile of strychnine hidden in his boot. He would not have allowed himself to soil his pants while he dangled from a rope.

29

The months following Billy's death were like a never-ending Irish wake. At the post office or around Fort Sumner, everyone had a story to tell about Billy. The time Hugo Villarreal had an infected leg. Billy borrowed a wagon and took Hugo to Las Vegas to see the only real doctor this side of Santa Fe. He stayed with Hugo for three days and paid the doctor bill. When Billy brought the old man safely back to the fort, a small fiesta was held in his honor. Not Hugo's. In Billy's honor.

There was the time Billy saw Jose Calderon's pinto tied outside Beaver Smith's saloon. Billy went inside, expecting to see Calderon. Instead, Billy found a man he knew from White Oaks had ridden the horse into Sumner. Billy ordered a beer and decided how he would confront the horse thief. Billy finally decided to go outside and steal the horse back and return it to Calderon at Frank Lobato's sheep camp. That way the horse thief would find himself drunk and on foot.

There were stories about Billy showing up at bible class on Sunday mornings. He would wear his best white shirt and make himself useful as he handed out the hymnbooks. Billy had little interest in the scriptures, but he loved to sing the songs.

A week after Billy's death, a wagon stopped at the post office on its way south. When I stepped outside, I saw a young Mexican woman with an old man. As I walked toward them, I recognized Hortencia from Padre Polaco's cantina at Puerto de Luna. The viejo next to her was the man Billy had defended against the gun hand from Texas.

When I asked Hortencia what had brought them so far from home, she said that they were going to Fort Sumner to place flowers on Billy's grave. She said that Billy was the only boy she would ever love. She and her father would never forget him. I guessed that the old man did not know English. He simply looked at me and nodded.

A few weeks later, I talked with John Poe,

who was on his way from White Oaks to Texas. He did not seem at all satisfied that he had played a part in Billy's death. He confided that Garrett was ready to give up the search and return to Lincoln. Poe had encouraged Garrett to confer with Pete Maxwell. Poe said there were many things that still troubled him about that night. Poe wanted no part of any fanfare that might be accorded him.

The following week, Yginio Salazar stopped by to post a letter to Lincoln while he was on his way to Las Vegas. He explained that he had ridden with the Regulators. During the five day siege in Lincoln, he had been with Billy and the others in the McSween house. When they made their break for the Rio Bonito, Salazar had been shot and left for dead. One of Dolan's drunken men stepped on his chest and was ready to shoot him in the head. Another man told him not to waste a bullet.

Late that night, Salazar managed to crawl to his sister-in-law's house. The next day Jimmy Dolan's men, who had followed his trail of blood, discovered him. They were going to kill him, but the doctor from Fort Stanton stood in their way.

Salazar said that Billy was always the clearest thinker in the whole outfit. In their tightest scrapes, Salazar had never seen any sign of fear in the young fighter. During the three years that they had known each other, what impressed Salazar the most was Billy's kindness to poor people.

Salazar confessed that he was the one who took care of Billy at Las Tablas for three days after Billy's escape from jail in Lincoln. He asked me to keep that information under my hat. After they removed the leg irons, Billy camped above the house. He said Billy was undecided about going to Mexico. He worried that he would not know anyone there and there would be no way to make money. Against Salazar's advice, Billy finally decided to return to Fort Sumner.

In a conversation with Jesus Silva at Fort Sumner, he told me that he had been with Billy just before he was shot. He said that he was standing under a cottonwood tree when Billy strolled by. Billy had just ridden into town. He was hot and tired. They decided to have a beer together. Billy said he was going to a nearby house to get something to eat.

Later, when Silva heard shots, he rushed over to the Maxwell house and found Garrett, Maxwell and two deputies on the outside of Pete's room. Garrett told Silva to take a candle

276

and go in and see if the Kid was dead. Silva entered the room along with Delvina Maxwell, the Navajo servant.

There on the floor, they found Billy. He was face down. They turned him over and saw that he was dead. Delvina began to cry as she cursed Pat Garrett, who had just come into the room. Until that time, Garrett was not sure that it was Billy lying on the floor.

Pete Maxwell suggested that they take the body to the carpenters shop. Silva and three other Mexican men carried him to the empty room and laid him on a bench. The women placed a circle of candles around him. Silva then constructed a wooden box that would serve as a coffin.

Silva said when he found Billy on the floor there was a knife next to his right hand. There was no gun. Silva maintained that Billy was unarmed when he was shot. Silva said that he later found Billy's gun belt and revolver hanging on a nail inside the door at the home of Celsa Gutierrez. If this were true, it would explain why Billy would have ducked into Maxwell's room for cover.

I located Delvina Maxwell that same afternoon. When I said I needed to talk with her, she stared into my eyes so intently that I had to look away. I asked her about the night that she found Billy. Her story squared with Jesus Silva's. She said there was only a knife next to the body. She said the son-of-a-bitch Garrett did not give her little boy a chance.

That was enough for me. Jesus Silva and Delvina Maxwell had no reason to lie. On the other hand, Pat Garrett's political ambitions in the territory would have ended if it were known that Billy was unarmed. Garrett would have been treated as a pariah everywhere he traveled.

Garrett had spent the night with Pete Maxwell and his two deputies, holed up in the Maxwell home. None of them would prosper if it was known that Billy was unarmed. A friend of Billy's might have later shot Garrett or Maxwell. They would have spent the rest of their days looking over their shoulders.

The cleanest solution would be for all four of them to agree to the story that Billy and Garrett had faced off and Garrett shot first. When they convened the coroner's jury the next morning, all four of these respectable men would provide the same account. The jury's conclusion would be that the killing was justifiable homicide.

Some weeks later, I had an interesting conversation with Ash Upson. He was the postmaster at Roswell. He had worked for newspapers from New York City to Cincinnati and all over the West. We talked for a long while about the newspaper business. We compared the most interesting stories we had covered. We could have swapped tales of the newspaper wars for two days and not run out of material.

Upson mentioned that he and Pat Garrett were going to collaborate on a book about Billy the Kid. This revelation did not surprise me. Garrett always had a new scheme to make money. What better opportunity than a book written by the man who killed Billy the Kid.

I knew before the book was written that Garrett would be the hero of the piece. He would be portrayed as the uncompromising lawman that rid New Mexico Territory of all of its dangerous outlaws. I doubted that there would an account that was anywhere near the truth about the executions of Tom O'Folliard, Charlie Bowdre and Billy Bonney. The circumstances of their deaths were not unlike the buffalo that Garrett had killed from a safe distance.

I was tempted to ask Upson if he knew that Billy was unarmed when he was killed by the great lawman. I decided to let that sleeping dog lie. It was at this moment that I decided that

279

someone would have to tell the other side of the story. The press and the dime novels could spread their silly tales, but I knew the other side.

Upson began to tell of his time in Silver City when he had boarded at the home of Catherine Antrim. I was anxious to hear the details. Upson said that Billy's stepfather would disappear for weeks in search of a silver strike. Catherine would take in laundry and bake pies to make ends meet. In addition, she would take in several boarders in her thirty by thirty foot cabin.

Upson had nothing but kind words to say about Billy's mother. She was always in good spirits. She would greet him with a smile and a joke. He said that when she and Billy would go to a dance, the man at the door would wave them in with a smile. Catherine was the main attraction. She would dazzle the crowd with her dance steps as she circled the floor with her young son.

Upson insisted that Billy was the spitting image of his mother, from his blue eyes and fair skin to his outgoing ways. He said that either of them could make a friend in an instant. He said that Catherine was a very handsome woman. She had an honest look about her. Upson said that her acts of charity around Silver City were legendary.

According to Upson, there was no undertaker in Silver City at the time of Catherine's death. Mrs. Truesdell prepared the body and a service was held at the Antrim cabin. He said that Billy betrayed no emotion as he stared into the coffin. Upson described the boy as a lost soul. The coffin was taken to the cemetary in the back of a freight wagon. Upson estimated that there were nearly a hundred people at her burial.

In the fall of 1881, all the newspapers carried stories of a great gun battle that had occurred in the streets of Tombstone, Arizona. The Earp brothers and Doc Holliday had faced down the Clantons and McLaurys. Ike Clanton and Billy Claiborne had fled from the fight while Billy Clanton and the McLaury brothers had been killed. Two of the Earps and Doc Holliday had been wounded.

I remembered what Padre Polaco had told me about Ike Clanton while Billy and I were in Puerto de Luna. He said there was a stolen livestock operation that ran from Clanton in Arizona to John Kinney in Mesilla and up to the Texas Panhandle. In Arizona and New Mexico, it appeared that salad days of stealing livestock were coming to an end.

The following April, the headlines were all

about Jesse James being killed in Missouri. A friend named Bob Ford had shot him in the back. According the papers, Ford's intention was to collect the considerable reward money on the famous outlaw.

James had traveled to Las Vegas when the railhead reached there in 1880. In a chance meeting with Billy Bonney, James had encouraged Billy to join a new gang that he was putting together. Billy declined. As they ate supper, Billy explained that robbing trains and banks was not his line of work. Billy was the small thinker of the two. He preferred to work the edges of the big cattle herds when he needed money. In the end, Jesse James managed to live nine months longer than Billy.

In May 1882, The Las Vegas Daily Optic printed a story about the Widow McSween. She had traveled to Las Vegas to settle a matter concerning her late husband's estate. She was invited to have dinner with Miguel Otero, whose father ran the San Miguel National Bank. A reporter from the Optic was allowed to join them in order to hear her version of the war in Lincoln and the now infamous Billy the Kid. Here are Susan McSweens words:

I should like to speak of the time the

Murphy men poisoned one of the men who was working on the new store building for Tunstall. The Murphy men tried in every way to get the carpenter to quit his work, but with no success. One day the carpenter was given a drink by one of Murphy's men and a few moments later, he dropped dead.

I was in our house when the Murphy crowd set fire to it. Since the house was of adobe, the fire did not make rapid progress as it ate its way around from the from the northwest corner. I would have stayed in the house until the last wall had fallen had not the boys who were there insisted that I leave.

I did go back and forth between the house and Colonel Dudley's camp. I found the colonel in his tent drinking whiskey with John Kinney, one of the worst characters in the territory. They used the vilest language while I pleaded with Colonel Dudley to save my burning house and the lives of those in it.

John Kinney, in a bragging manner, told me he had killed fourteen men and would make the number fifteen when he killed my husband. The day after my home was burned to the ground and five of those in it lost their lives, several of the Murphy crowd went into the Tunstall store and looted thousands of dollars worth of merchandise.

Billy often said he loved Mr. Tunstall more than any man he ever knew. I have always believed that if Mr. Tunstall had lived, Billy would have become a valuable citizen. He was a remarkable boy, far above the average of the young men of those times. The best people of Lincoln County were his friends and admirers. He was a wholehearted boy who was kind and loyal to all those deserving such a return from him.

The Kid was universally liked, especially by the native citizens. They loved him because he was kind and considerate to them and took much pleasure in helping them and providing for their wants. He thought nothing of mounting his horse and riding all night for a doctor or for medicine to relieve the suffering of a sick person.

Billy was a graceful and beautiful dancer and when in the company of a woman, he was at all times extremely polite and respectful. He was neat and careful about his personal appearance.

He was always a great favorite with women and at a dance he was in constant demand. Yet with it all, he was entirely free of conceit or vanity. It was just natural for him to be a perfect gentleman.

Of course, Billy killed his two guards, Bell and Olinger. Self-preservation is the first law of nature. He did not want to kill Bell, but was forced to shoot as they fought for the gun. The killing of Bob Olinger was approved by everyone, including Olinger's mother. She told me that her son had been a murderer at heart from the cradle up until the moment of his death. She admitted he had gotten his just desserts when Billy shot him.

Billy often told me that Pat Garrett was a cattle rustler and had stolen many a head of cattle from the Canadian while he was living at Fort Sumner. It was Captain J. C. Lea who got Garrett to turn traitor to Billy. For doing so, Garrett was made sheriff of Lincoln County. The only condition was to get the Kid, which Garrett did in his usual way. Pat Garrett's courage is much overrated. He is a coward at heart. He only shot when he had the advantage or, as they say, had the drop on his opponent. It is said that

every man he has killed was shot without
warning.

Tom O'Folliard, one of Billy's
associates, was another good-natured,
rollicking boy, always singing and full of
fun. He and Billy were much alike in this
manner, but Billy was superior in every
way. In truth, Billy was quite alone in his
class. I could not help liking the boy,
although I did not approve of his mode of
livelihood. I suppose he felt justified in
stealing cattle from the large ranches that
had pushed the native people from their
land.

I gave Harold Early credit for having the
nerve to print this story. It would not be well
received in Santa Fe. The favorable account of
William Bonney flew in the face of everything
that was being written about him. The
condemnation of the great Pat Garrett would
anger the big cattlemen and powerful politicians
who supported him. Only Harold had the
backbone to pick at this scab.

The territorial papers had been quick to
attribute twenty-one killings to Billy the Kid.
One for every year of his life. By my count, it
was four. Cahill, the blacksmith who was

beating the tar out of Billy in a saloon at Fort Grant. Joe Grant, alias Texas Red, who tried to shoot Billy in the back of the head in Bob Hargrove's saloon. Deputies Bell and Olinger when Billy broke out of jail in Lincoln. I thought that was enough killing for a boy just old enough to vote.

During the Lincoln County War, Billy had plenty of company shooting from his side. There was plenty of death to go around. I have read that more than two hundred people lost their lives during the violence in the southern part of the territory. To my knowledge, Billy was the only man who had been tried and sentenced to hang.

30

After nearly five years at our lonely outpost on the Pecos, we received notice that the government was closing the post office at the end of July. In truth, life had become tedious on the little knoll that overlooked the Pecos River. Fort Sumner was much less interesting without Billy and the Regulators. The moneyed interests had won out. The days of the free riders were over.

I wrote to Harold Early in Las Vegas. He agreed to hire me as a reporter for the Daily Optic. He warned that there would be a terrible price to pay. He said I would have to grovel at his feet on a daily basis and tell him what a great man he was. Harold thought he might also be able to find a teaching position for Susan.

There was no thought of our returning to

Chicago. Joe Finnegan still held out hope that I would one day take over the operation of his tannery. As much as I liked Joe, I had no inclination to spend the rest of my days down wind of the Union Stockyards.

Susan and I had become very fond of New Mexico. We would not trade the kind, dry weather for the cold wind blowing in off Lake Michigan. We had been spoiled by the clear blue skies and the fine Mexican food. We enjoyed an easy camaraderie with the Hispano people. The pace of life in New Mexico had come to suit us.

It had been one year since Billy was killed. Time had stopped in these parts while everyone remembered Billy. Not a week went by without someone coming by the post office with a new tale to tell. Anything that had ever happened around Fort Sumner paled in comparison to the memory of William Bonney.

I was certain that Pete Maxwell was relieved to have regained control of Fort Sumner. Paulita had been sent to live with relatives up on the Cimarron. Nasaria Yerby and Abrana Garcia had each given birth to a baby daughter, but neither infant had survived. There was sorrow in every direction. A pall had been spread over the little village.

Susan and I were reluctant to abandon our comfortable adobe home. In the summer, we would open the windows and doors and let the evening breeze blow through the house. In the winter, the corner fireplace kept the little adobe warm in the coldest weather. The slow moving Pecos curved around the house on its way south. Most of the folks at Fort Sumner were our friends.

While Susan loaded the last of her personal belongings into the wagon, Lonesome Joe was at her side. He was confused by the disruption. The thought of losing his bed by the fireplace and his bowl on the kitchen floor was probably more than the old spotted dog could bear.

I sat across the road on a bench in front of the empty post office. As I leaned back against the wall, a strong wind had come up from the south. The dark clouds moving toward us meant that heavy summer rains were on the way. We would probably have to wait out the storm before we headed for Las Vegas.

As I looked in the direction of the storm, a huge tumbleweed came rolling up the center of the road. As it blew past me, I could see Billy gallop by on Gracie, his tall grey mare. He was wearing the tattered red serape and his black sombrero.

290

The wind faded for a moment and the tumbleweed paused on the road, just beyond where I was sitting. Billy turned and waved his sombrero. Adios. He had that toothy smile that had made so many friends during his stay along the Pecos.

The wind picked up again. The tumbleweed veered left and sailed toward the river. I watched as Gracie raced across the short grass with Billy low on her back. When the rolling weed disappeared, I realized that Billy had no more chance of choosing the direction of his life than that tumbleweed. When John Tunstall was killed, a gust of wind sent Billy in a new direction.

I remembered something Billy had said while he sipped his tea during our first visit. He said a horse could spend its days in front of a plow or a hay wagon or it could try to race a hole through the wind. For three years along the Pecos, Billy had chased that hole in the wind. On a warm night in July, in a dark room at Fort Sumner, that hole in the wind was closed forever.